Redemption

Somerset University

Ruby Vincent

Published by Ruby Vincent, 2021.

Prologue

Maverick

"Sawyer, look. He's waking up."

My ear pressed to a hard, lined surface. A rhythmic *thump, thump, thump* sounded beneath me, and a sudden jolt lifted me and smacked my head on the floor. The knock flooded clarity into my fogged mind. I was lying on a moving surface.

I went to grab my aching head and nothing happened. I tried again, straining in my bonds.

"Easy, Rick."

That voice. Hot, molten rage burned away the last of the haze. *I knew that fucking voice.*

"It's just a bit of rope and chloroform." Hands grabbed and flipped me over. I gazed up into Sawyer's and Aiden's eyes. "Don't look so betrayed. This was the only way."

It was dark. Aiden and Sawyer were the sole figures I made out clearly. Another bump and the jolt kicked us up.

Van, a voice supplied. *I'm in the back of a van.*

"What the fuck... do you think you're doing?"

"It's simple really," said Sawyer. "Once we explain it all, you'll agree."

I glared at him. Less than a week ago, I sat next to his hospital bed while he fought tears and rivaled Casper the Friendly Ghost in complexion. Right then he looked ready to run a marathon. "You were sick..."

"As a dog," he agreed. "Did you know, you can measure the exact amount needed for someone to overdose without dying? All I had to do was fuck with Bebop, wait for you to show up to fix it, and then spill our story while you thought I was weak and vulnerable enough to tell the truth."

He lied? It was all a damn lie?

"Why?"

Aiden nodded, smiling that vile smile. I swore then and there I'd knock out every one of those teeth. "I told you it's simple. You see, it all started when I was alerted that someone hacked my encryption. Me," he repeated. "No one hacks me. It didn't take me long to trace the source back to you, and by then, I was intrigued.

"I knew what you were after. Ezra had Valentina suspicious of me and therefore you were too. I might've ignored you like I did the two of them, but anyone with your skills was someone I had to know."

"So, I joined your flag football team," Sawyer said, "and robotics. I did my best but you're not the easiest person to befriend."

"Didn't matter because I was working on something just for you," Aiden added. "You were looking for a mystery. Debauchery. The evil, cunning reason behind Sawyer's disappearance, so that's what we gave you. The club."

"Got lazy with that part. Didn't bother giving it a real name," Sawyer said.

"Cut me a break." They sounded like two guys kicking back for a chat. "I invented a secret society out of thin air, got the guys to help, fashioned you a fake drug and alcohol problem, and orchestrated it so on a dark, random night, Maverick Beaumont would walk up to another van all alone thinking he was safe."

"Why?!" I roared.

He shrugged. "I didn't have a choice. I had to fix a mistake. Playing football with you? We had to witness your fitness and stamina. Tossing poker chips and asking you *the question*. We found another way to give you the test." He tapped his skull. "To see how you reason. What you do when holding a bad hand. And club parties? Hello, bonding activities."

Aiden leaned over me, peering into my huge eyes. It was me. It was a trap from the moment Sawyer stepped into my elevator.

And I didn't see it.

"Somehow, we missed you." Aiden's intense gaze flayed me, stripping away my defenses and laying me bare. "Maverick Beaumont. It should've been you who walked through our door. Not Lennox. You," he whispered, "were meant to be one of us. A true Sam. And now, pledge, you will be."

My lips twisted. "Why in the fuck would I want to be one of you?"

He grinned back. "That's the best part. You'll find out exactly why in about ten hours. No more tricks. No more games. We're taking you to the same place Sawyer, Teagan, and so many Sallys and Sams have gone before. You'll find out why I have to do what I do, and when you come back, you'll help me continue what our very first president started all those years ago."

"Never. Going. To. Happen."

"Sawyer said the same thing," he sang.

"I did," Sawyer said. "Went down cursing, swearing, and promising on my mother's life. But I came around in the end. That's the thing, Rick. One way or another, we always give in." Sawyer reached behind him. "We've got a long drive."

He held up a cloth and a single brown bottle.

"You should get some sleep."

My shouts echoed through the van.

I yelled why. I yelled until I couldn't shout anymore.

Chapter One

"Mommy, what's wrong?"

"Nothing's wrong, baby." I fought to keep the panic out of my voice. "Daddy must've gotten confused and went home with someone else. Stay here with your toy."

I handed Adam his giraffe and kissed his forehead. He busied himself with playing while I walked a few feet from the car and called home. Ryder answered on the second ring.

"Val," he said. "On your way home?"

"Ryder, he's not here!" The dam broke, letting the worry free. "I called him. I talked to him. He knew I was picking him up, but he's not here."

"Whoa, slow down. What's going on?"

"Maverick isn't here," I cried. "Cydney said he got off the bus and went to speak to Sawyer. I'm standing in an empty parking lot. Maverick's gone!"

I heard a noise on his end, then heavy footsteps. "Is he gone, or is he in the bathroom or something? He just got off a long bus ride."

The question pierced my fog. "You're right. I didn't think of that." I whipped around, scanning for open buildings. "I have Adam with me. We'll look around and see if we find him."

"I'm on my way."

I carried Adam to every building surrounding the quad—bypassing the ones that were locked and poking my head in the bathrooms of the others. Ryder pulled up as I returned to the car.

"No," I said, running into his arms. "Something's wrong, Ryder. I can feel it."

"Take Adam home."

"I'm not—"

"Val." Ryder shifted his gaze to Adam. His green eyes were wide and staring. "Take him home," he said gently. "I'll stay and wait for the police."

"Police?" I rasped.

"If he knew you were coming, he wouldn't have left with anyone else. Something is wrong, and we're not waiting to find out what. I'll call you. Let you know what's going on the whole time."

It took more prodding, but Ryder finally got me into the car. I drove off with one name in my head.

Sawyer.

"ARE YOU CERTAIN YOU didn't get your wires crossed?"

"How many times do I have to repeat myself? We talked while he was on the bus. He knew I was coming to get him. There's no reason he'd have gone off with someone else without telling me."

"Hmm." Officer Mylow bobbed his head, scribbling something else in his notepad.

I didn't make hanging around police stations a habit. Still, I had a feeling Evergreen Police Station wasn't the norm. Movies and television shows conjured visions of scuffed tile, cluttered bulletin boards, broken blinds, and coffee-stained desks. This place was more a high-end department store minus the clothes. High ceilings, drapes on the large windows, large oak desks, and plush bench chairs like the one Ryder and I were sitting on.

"Here you are, ma'am." The receptionist placed a mug of tea and honey packet in front of me. "Can I get you anything else?"

"No, thank you," I said distractedly. "After he got off the bus, he went to speak to a guy named Sawyer Burn." I tapped his pad. "That's Sawyer Burn. The same guy previously reported missing. It's not a coincidence that Burn drops off the face of the earth, and then Maverick disappears after talking to him."

"Ma'am, I understand this is a stressful situation," said Mylow, "but it hasn't yet been twenty-four hours. Your friend might still turn up with a reasonable explanation for his absence."

"Boyfriend."

"Excuse me?"

"He's not my friend, he's my boyfriend."

"Oh." Mylow flicked to Ryder. He opened his mouth, thought better of it, and closed it.

He was a young, pleasant-looking fellow with plump cheeks and a thick head of sandy hair. I imagined him as one of those small, seaside village officers whose most serious arrests in a year were locking a few drunk-and-disorderlies in the tank to dry out.

This is the man searching for Maverick.

"I keep saying," I continued. "There isn't a reasonable explanation. Nothing that's been happening since I joined that damn sorority has been reasonable. Something is going on and Maverick's gotten caught up in it. You need to bring Aiden Connelly in for questioning. And don't let his slippery ass talk his way out of here. He knows what's going on."

"Aiden Connelly," he repeated. "The man you mentioned earlier in connection with Mr. Burn's disappearance."

"That's right."

"Mr. Burn, who fell off the face of the earth and returned unharmed to kidnap your boyfriend on the orders of the man who held him against his will?"

I stiffened. The cocked brow and derisive twist to his lips were anything but pleasant.

"Watch your fucking mouth," Ryder hissed. "If we knew what the hell was going on, we wouldn't be sitting here wasting our time with you."

Mylow's smirk melted away. "Mr. Shea, I didn't mean—"

"I know exactly what you meant. Mocking someone reporting a serious crime. Is that how you treat everyone who comes in here?"

"Of course not," he sputtered.

"Then, open your ears, close your mouth, and muster up some professionalism. Sawyer Burn was snatched off the street by a person or people in a black van during Valentina's freshman year. He was sent to that van by Aiden Connelly. He told him he was bringing in a keg. This was after an overheard conversation where Connelly told his brothers Sawyer would be gone soon.

"After Sawyer disappeared, Aiden made loaded comments but admitted to nothing. The police got word that Burn was safe with his family and refused to look any further. Then, Burn showed up like nothing happened, acting like he didn't know why anyone was worried.

"Whatever happened to Burn while he was gone, we acknowledge he wasn't physically harmed. But he was— Do you hear me? He *was* taken by surprise that night and loaded into a van like a couch they found on the sidewalk. Last I checked, that's still a crime even if he decides he's over it a year later.

"Now Maverick is gone, he's not answering his phone, and he was last seen in the company of someone who disappeared under strange circumstances." Ryder smacked the desk, nearly popping the man out of his seat. "Do you need me to keep spelling it out for you? Or are you going to get off your ass and find Sawyer Burn and Aiden Connelly?"

Chin trembling, Mylow swallowed hard. "I understand your concerns due to the circumstances you've stated. I will speak to Mr. Burn as he seems to be the last person who saw Mr. Beaumont. He may have light to shed on the situation. Please, go home and wait for me to contact you with news. I urge you not to take matters into your own hands."

Mylow got up to leave before us. Apparently, our interview was over.

"I do love that Brillo pad side of you when I'm not on the other end of it."

"The guy's a moron. We didn't walk in here first thing in the morning for fun." He laced our fingers together. "We had to report it to the police, but fuck not taking matters into our own hands. I've got our entire security team on this. There's a guy in IT I pay six figures a year who's going to hack into Maverick's phone and see if we can track it. We will find him, Valentina."

"I know we will." I squeezed his hand. "I won't allow myself to believe any different."

Two Weeks Later

"VAL, I'M SURE HE'S okay."

I jerked and closed out of the photo I was viewing of me and Maverick. I shoved my phone in my pocket.

"It's been two weeks, Sofia, and they haven't found a trace of him." My lips curled. "Aiden and Sawyer are gone too. There's no one to talk to. There's nothing I can do but sit around like an idiot, waiting for something to happen. Maverick needs me."

Sofia climbed in bed with me. Maverick's bed of course. I slept in it every night—part of me hoping I'd wake in the middle of the night and find him warm and solid next to me like so many times before.

"Then let's not sit around waiting for something to happen. Zeta Rho gave you a leave of absence to focus on Maverick."

"They gave me a leave of absence because I pelted Jade with questions every time I saw her," I snapped. "She practically kicked me out of the house under the excuse of 'lightening my load during this difficult time.'"

"That might not be a bad thing, Val. If Jade knows what's going on, she's not going to come clean, and being around her always wondering if she's holding something back would drive you crazy."

I lifted my head from the pillow. "What are you saying? It's better that woman has free rein in my house to disappear half the sisters from their beds and keep smiling the next morning like nothing happened?"

"I'm there, Val. You know I wouldn't let that happen. And if it did, I'd scream holy hell until someone took that kidnapper away and locked her up."

A fraction of my anger leeched away. I sank into the sheets. "I know you would. I'm just frustrated. I feel like I've been shouting for weeks, months, years, and no one is listening to me." My throat clogged. "Now when it really matters and Maverick is in trouble, all I keep thinking is I should've shouted louder."

Sofia shook her head. "You can't think like that. You did everything you could to get people to listen, but somehow, we were always a step behind." Her brows drew together. "We both can agree this has been going on for a long time. Much longer than Leighton or Aiden. If the Sam and Sally disappearances over the years are linked, then whoever is doing this has gotten away with it for a long time.

"They must've run into questioning sisters, worried parents, and cops before. Despite that, they've managed to get around all of them without anyone figuring out what's happening in those picture-perfect houses."

"What are you saying?" I asked, brows furrowing.

"I'm saying, it's not that you didn't shout loud enough. It might be that we're dealing with someone who figured out a long time ago how to make sure no one listens."

I shivered, clutching the blankets tighter. "Goodness, Sof. Is that supposed to reassure me?"

"Yes," she said firmly. "Because the problem isn't that we're going about this wrong. We're doing exactly what we're supposed to do, but a serial kidnapper becomes one because they learn how to evade cops, parents, and private security."

I began to speak and stopped myself. Closing my mouth, I turned over what she said.

"You're right," I replied. "Whatever's behind the façade of Zeta Rho Sigma and Nu Alpha Theta has existed long before we set foot on that campus. It's like Evergreen. The Spades were experts at covering their tracks. Normal rules didn't apply."

"Is this like Evergreen? Are we dealing with the same thing?"

Sitting up, I leaned on the headboard. "How can we be? This isn't an exclusive boarding school out in the woods. This is a university with thousands of students from all over the world enrolled."

"If we're talking about all of Somerset," she said, "yes. But if we're talking about two exclusive Greek houses overseen by men and women who must know more than they're saying..." Sofia let the rest hang in the air.

"I understand. We can't play by the same rules." I tightened my fists. "And if you want the truth, I stopped playing a long time ago. I'll do anything, Sofia. Tell me what you're thinking."

"We'll go out there and look for him ourselves. Maverick was tangled up in Aiden's club before he disappeared. We find that guy and *make him* tell us what he knows."

"Aiden's gone too."

"Are his parents?" she returned. "Girlfriend? Brothers? Sisters? Someone is going to know where he is. We'll follow the trail right back to him, then to Maverick."

I threw my arms around her. "Thank you. I don't know what I'd do without you, Sofia. I'm serious."

"You're not going to find out." She squeezed me till my bones cracked. "Don't lose hope, Val. That's not what you do."

"No, it isn't. What I do is bring bullies to their knees."

Someone cleared their throat. "Sofia, would you give us a minute?"

Ryder came inside the room. Sofia said bye and stepped out, leaving Ryder to lift me off the bed.

"What are you doing?"

"You're not staying in this room imagining the worst anymore. I caught the tail end of your conversation with Sofia. I'm not going to tell you it's too dangerous, or to stay away from these people. I wouldn't listen if it were me and you're ten times as stubborn."

"Ten times as stubborn as you is the Great Wall of China refusing to crumble after three thousand years. It's impossible to reach that level, but I'll get there in a second if it's for Maverick."

"Thank you for illustrating what I'm talking about." Ryder shut us in our room, bringing me to the couch. "My guy finally did it. Remotely hacked Maverick's phone."

I sat up straight. "And?"

Ryder shook his head. "Tracked it to a dumpster on the other side of campus. It's a dead end."

"Of course. A dead end we would've caught on sooner if Maverick's parents hadn't chosen now of all times to go on vacation. Were you able to reach them?"

"No. His parents have this thing about being unplugged on vacations. Otherwise, his father opens his laptop to check one email and two hours later he's in a virtual meeting with shareholders. They don't bother to bring phones or laptops with them anymore. And still, his mom won't forgive us for not letting her know."

"I'll stop by again today to see if they're back." I hugged my knees to my chest, dropping my chin on them. "What are we dealing with here, Ryder? What are they doing to him?"

"At least we know Teagan and Sawyer weren't hurt while they were *gone*. It doesn't look like that is what this is about."

"No, they were just inducted into some kind of cult that keeps murderers like Leighton around! Forgive me if I'm not reassured." I groaned. "It's even worse that I became president to find the truth and protect the sisters, but I couldn't protect my own boyfriend. I'm even more lost than before. Any chance I had of learning things quietly is gone. Jade knows I'm not fooled."

"Then, it's like Sofia said. We stop being quiet and asking nicely. Someone in your house knows what's going on." Ryder gave me a tender kiss. "They will tell us whether they want to or not."

"I know who to start with."

THAT NIGHT, RYDER, Jaxson, Ezra, Adam, and I walked along the property. The place was a park, botanical garden, and meadow onto itself. Acres and acres of green, and Pepper was sniffing every inch of it. Adam let go of me and Ryder to chase after the puppy.

"It's his birthday coming up," Ezra remarked. He slid his hand into mine. "There's been a lot of talk about jungle themes and everyone in his class coming. He's pretty much planning this party without us."

I cracked a smile watching Adam. "I can't believe he's turning seven." My smile dimmed. "Any more than I can believe we're planning this party without Maverick. He asks me every night why his dad isn't here to read him his bedtime story."

"We don't have to throw the party if you're not up to it, Val," Jaxson said.

He walked ahead of us along the garden path, holding Pepper's leash. My gaze fell on his rump in those jeans. All of us had grown from that fateful first year in Evergreen Academy. My guys had always been too handsome for their own good.

Jaxson burst blood vessels with a direct look at his grin. Ezra was a lethal mix of dark eyes and smoldering intensity. Ryder was so pristinely beautiful like Michelangelo's David preserved in Carrara marble. Years later, and my men had only grown more devastating.

Jaxson had filled out in every way. His shirts strained to hold him. The leather jackets he'd taken to wearing did nothing to hide it.

Ezra had fully grown into the look that would carry him into middle age. Sharp cheekbones, full lips, professional outfits that hid the dangerous, passionate man underneath. He was one of those guys destined to be a silver fox. I'd be fighting women off him for the rest of our lives.

And Ryder. He was the model on an office romance cover—sexy, authoritative, and a man to put you on your knees with one command. One glance at him, I saw curly-headed babies with smoky eyes and mischief in their smile.

These were my loves. My guys. My family. And without Maverick, we weren't whole.

"We are throwing the party," I stated. "Adam's birthday is in three weeks. Maverick will be home by then. Until he is, I want everything to be normal for our son. It won't do any good scaring him." I took a deep breath and let it go. "Jungle theme it is. We'll hire someone to entertain the kids with snakes, iguanas, and animals. The kids can dress up like adventurers, and we'll set up an obstacle course playland in the yard. We need something good to look forward to right now."

That night, we tucked Adam in bed and drew the covers over him and Pepper. She had a basket at the foot of his bed, but in the mornings, we'd walk in and find her curled up next to him. We stopped fighting it.

Cara scurried inside and joined the party, lying out on Adam's pillow. I moved the cat to his other side.

"Excited for your party, baby?"

"Yes! Can we have a giraffe at my party?"

"I wish, but they wouldn't fit through the door," I said. "We can go to the zoo and see one though."

"Okay. The lions too."

"We're going to see *all* the animals," I cried, throwing out my hands.

Adam giggled. "Will Daddy be here for my party?"

Adam called them all Daddy, but this time we had no trouble figuring out who he was talking about.

"Of course he will. Daddy wouldn't miss it."

Smiling, Adam flipped over and threw his arm over Cara, content to sleep. We kissed him good night one by one. Ryder's phone buzzed as he bent over Adam.

"Night, son."

He drew back, checked his phone, and nodded at me. I wasn't sure what that meant.

Ryder stepped out while I quietly tidied Adam's room, hoping for once it meant something good.

RYDER

"Jacob," I answered.

"We have that background on Kessler, Ortega, Connelly, Burn, and the men Maverick befriended during those poker games."

"Anything stand out?"

"Nothing out of the ordinary. Kessler and Ortega do not have unexplained absences in their backgrounds. The research Miss Moon did into the dropouts was helpful. We've looked into them ourselves and haven't had any luck tracing them outside of their appearances the night of the charity fundraiser."

"You're calling me to tell me you have nothing."

"On the contrary," Jacob said calmly. "I'm calling to tell you there's no doubt something is very wrong here. In today's age, it's impossible to not leave a trace. Maverick Technologies is a billion-dollar company for that reason. Governments, companies, and contractors pay all they can afford to protect their information as successfully as a couple of dropouts from the local university.

"Something is going on," he said. "Whoever took Mr. Beaumont is well-funded and fanatical about not getting caught. Sawyer mentioned an athletic angle. A program to bring athletes to their full potential. There could be some truth in that."

My brows furrowed. "Why do you say that?"

"Because—excuse me—the pattern so far does not point to a serial killer or sexual sadist. Teagan, Sawyer, and Maverick are different genders, races, hair colors, etc. The only thing that appears to connect them is their intelligence and athleticism."

Drifting further from Adam's room, my mind ran a mile a minute. Jacob had a point. One I should've seen before. This was more than a warped nut with a fetish.

There had to be a reason they took Maverick—the son of a wealthy family and boyfriend of a woman suspicious of them. Whoever "them" was.

Maverick was worth the risk. So he had to possess some quality they wanted, and looking at their past victims would've told me that. It may even have told me Maverick was in trouble before it was too late.

I gripped the banister, a growl of frustration leaking through my teeth.

This is my fault.

I hadn't been involved in the secrets bringing Val's sorority down other than to tell her to stay out of it. I should've been in that damn basement, playing Connelly's games. I should've helped Val out of that pool and thrown Connelly and his buddies in it.

I stood by while Valentina and Maverick fought a battle with hidden enemies on all sides, and now my brother paid the price.

"Send me everything you have," I ordered. "I mean everything. Someone in those houses knows exactly what's going on, and we're going to make them talk."

"Ryder, might I suggest you let us handle the questioning."

"No. I have to— *We* have to do this ourselves. Maverick's family. I won't sit by fielding phone calls and waiting for updates while that grinning freak Aiden screws with him."

"Of course," he said easily. "I'll send you the information and more as we continue. Although, I will make another suggestion."

"What?" I gritted.

"We were able to get as far as we did because Valentina's access granted the privileges she was looking for. It's best she doesn't lose them now." Jacob said it in his usual even tone, but the message was clear.

Don't do anything that'll get Val kicked out of the Sallys and our only source of information lost.

"We know what we're doing."

"About what?" Val came up behind me. "Work or Maverick?"

"Maverick," I told her. "Bye, Jacob. Send me that information."

"What about Maverick?" Valentina asked as I hung up.

I towed her to our bedroom and peeled her clothes off after I shut the door. It'd been a long two weeks, and if we were having this conversation, we were doing it in a hot bath.

"The other people who disappeared from the Sallys and Sams, do you know their majors? What they looked like? If they played sports? Anything like that."

"I have the names. It should be easy enough to look up."

She didn't stop me taking her into the bathroom and running the tub. I let her take over pouring the bubbles she liked and getting the candles from under the sink. "Why?" she asked.

"Jacob thinks there's a reason they're taking these people in particular. Maybe the reason is exactly what Sawyer told Maverick. They're guinea pigs for a well-funded operation that needs men and women in peak physical condition."

A tiny wrinkle appeared between her brows.

"If you think about it, Maverick, Burn, and Kainer only have that in common. They took a huge risk taking someone like Maverick Beaumont." Anger licked at my self-control. "And it's going to be what finally exposes their asses. There must be a reason they decided Maverick was worth the hell I'll rain down on them."

Valentina took my hands, guiding me into the bath. "I've actually thought about this too. Why Maverick? He's not a Sam or an easy target." She looked away. "I admit, I thought he was punishing me. Punishing us for pissing off Aiden. He's an oily bastard and I'm sure wherever he is, he's enjoying thinking of me miserable without Maverick."

The undulating steam rose from the filling tub. Valentina chose sweet, rose-scented bubbles. They billowed from behind her, recalling the scene of Aphrodite emerging from the foam. She truly was the most beautiful creature I'd ever seen.

Even when she was sad.

Sorrow darkened her lily-green eyes and reflected the fears I couldn't say aloud. Maverick was fine. He had to be. Whatever our punishment was to be for pissing off Aiden Connelly, I refused to believe Maverick wouldn't be there when we got our revenge.

"But if this is some kind of program to create super athletes, why don't the Sams and Sallys post sign-ups in the kitchen and ask us to join like normal people!" she cried. "Who throws someone in the back of a van?"

"There's something about this that must be kept quiet," I mused aloud. "Sports is a four-hundred-billion-dollar-a-year industry. There must be a lot of money involved in this, because in some way, it always comes back to money."

"But this has been going on for years, Ryder." She propped her feet on my lap, leaning back as she massaged her temples. "It's been too long and too secretive to believe this is some simple trial to improve athletic performance. If we put aside for a minute that Aiden Connelly is a psychopath and everything he says can be discarded as a lie, we come back to Leighton.

"Leighton is up to her neck in this. If her *friends* are the same people we're dealing with, they cleaned up a body on her say-so. Who knows how many times they've done that?" Those green eyes pierced me through. "Who knows how many of the Sallys and Sams we can't find were cleaned up too?

"Teagan and Sawyer came back safe and sound because they're on board. By choice or blackmail, I don't know. But this is not harmless, Ryder, and you're not making me feel better by filling my head with theories you don't even believe in."

I said nothing. Just stared across the short distance as I rubbed her feet.

"You're right," I finally replied. "I don't believe it's harmless either. But I'm not going to stop trying to make you feel better. What's the alternative, Val? Accepting Sawyer killed him and called the cleanup crew?"

She winced. "No. Maverick is fine. I know he is," Val whispered. "I can feel it."

Leaning across, I shut the water off. Val caught me and wrapped her arms around me. I took Val with me, settling against the porcelain and holding her tight.

"I know two things, Val," I said. "Maverick is kicking ass wherever he is, fighting to get back home to you. And if he doesn't get to us first, we'll get to him."

She popped bubbles on my chest. "I know a third thing. Aiden Connelly will pay for this. He'll regret the day I set foot on Somerset campus."

"That's a given."

Val raised her head to meet my eyes. "You drew this bath to relax me, didn't you? So far, it's not working."

"Give me a hint. Would it help to describe the many violent acts we'll commit against Aiden and his cronies when this is over? Or a complete subject change?"

She laughed softly. A laugh over as quickly as it started, but still a laugh.

"Subject change, please. Aiden, Sawyer, Leighton, Reagan, the Sallys, and Sams are all I think about every second of every day. I was so excited to join the sorority and have a fun, normal four years with my best friend," she said. "A shadow's been cast over everything. Somerset. The sorority. Maverick. Us. I thought things would be different."

I wound her hair through my fingers, crushing under the truth of what she said.

"What's your favorite sex position?"

"What?" she cried, jerking up. "Ryder!"

"You asked for a subject change and you've got one. I expect an answer."

"That's the burning question on your mind?"

"I've always wondered."

Val's bubble-popping traveled lower. "Don't you know what I like?"

"Hot, dirty, and hard. You like scratches on my back. Hair matted. Lips swollen. Cock bulging and pussy weeping. You like when I tie you to the bed and refuse to free you till you've come the required number of times. You like when I smack that ass pink and tweak those perfect little nipples between my teeth."

Pink was the shade of choice dusting Valentina's cheeks. She bit her smile, giggling into my pecs.

"I know exactly what you like, Moon, but none of that tells me your favorite position."

If anything, she flushed deeper. "Remember that trip we took to Costa Rica?"

"Vividly."

Val traced a pattern at the base of the V between my legs. My muscles tightened to her attention, begging and pleading with her to continue much like Valentina did in Costa Rica.

"You tipped me over the couch and fucked me upside down. I came on my own face," she moaned. "That's my favorite position."

I hoisted her up. "Well, there'll be some slipping and sliding but I can make that happen."

Squealing, Val wiggled out of my hold. "I love you," she said, bringing me back down.

Our positions shifted and I lay on her, taking up the task of teasing. I nudged her legs apart, stroking her inner thigh.

"You should've said that's how you want it."

Val hummed. "Why? I love the unpredictable nature of our sexual encounters, Shea. Will he tip me upside down? Tie me up? Put me on my knees or my back? I never know and it makes it all the more delicious."

I sank inside her, cock swelling as her eyes fluttered shut and lips parted. This was the look that inspired the artist in me. I didn't know what I was going to do to Val when I got her naked either. I just saw that look and let my cock take over.

"Legs up."

She obeyed, draping her shapely, tan legs over the rim. One thing could be said by the Sallys' strict exercise regime. It was transforming her into a toned goddess who kept pace with me on my morning jogs without breaking a sweat. Made it so much easier when I veered, picked her up, and ducked us into the trees for an X-rated break.

I moved inside her. Slow, then fast, then slow as I found the right melody of breathy moans to stroke myself to.

Val clutched my shoulders. "Cock."

"Not yet."

"You don't get to tease me while you're cheering me up. Cock," she ordered.

"You're so fucking cute when you think you're in charge."

She wapped me with her foot. "I'm always in charge. I made you fall in love with me and devote the rest of your life to living in bliss with our family, puppy, and freaky sex."

I shrugged, picking up the pace. "Wasn't that hard. I was three-quarters of the way to dropping on my knee and pledging my wealth, love, and life from the moment I saw you."

"Only you can make the sweetest words into a comeback." She moved up my shoulders, trapped my chin, and stole a searing kiss. "Cock," she ordered.

"You first."

Val squeezed me at the root and didn't move except to tug me forward, pressing my tip to her clit. The lady knew what she wanted and she wanted it now. I plunged a third finger inside her.

My tongue darted out and tasted the sharp exhalation leaving her lips. I'd fuck this woman on her head for the rest of my life and thank all the deities for the honor.

Val kissed the tip of my nose. "Fuck me, baby," she whispered. "I need you."

I broke.

Cupping her neck, I arched her back and sank inside her. Val's thinly disguised triumph stirred something deep inside of me. She thought I lost this battle of wills, but there was no universe real or imagined where being balls deep in Valentina Moon was losing.

We were one entity—moving, writhing, groaning, splashing water over the rim. I felt her tighten, sensing the explosion coming like it was my own.

Swooping down, her nipple disappeared beneath my tongue. I flicked the hardening peak to her rising cries.

"Yes, Ryder. Just like that," she groaned. "Baby, you're incredible."

If I had low self-esteem, being with Valentina would cure me after a week. She knew how to make a man feel like he was as good as he *thought* he was.

Which is why I'll burn down the world if you stop smiling.

I bared my teeth in the midst of lifting her leg and drilling Val deeper.

Or I'll burn Nu Alpha Theta.

Val came shuddering beneath me. I held her jerking body in my hands, groans pouring from me as her clenching milked my cock of every drop.

She kissed me light and sweet. "Thank you. For a minute, I didn't feel like the world was collapsing in on me."

I stroked her cheek. "And now?"

Her sad smile said it all.

"We have to get him back, Ryder. We just have to."

"We will."

Chapter Two

*V*alentina

Monday morning, it was back to the routine. Adam had school, we had classes, and I had a houseful of women waiting for their president's return.

I woke Adam up, bathed and dressed him in his school uniform, then carried him downstairs for breakfast. A bowl of strawberry oatmeal and brown sugar whole-grain muffins awaited him at the table.

Normally, I preferred to make Adam's breakfast. Life had been so hectic since I stood alone in that empty parking lot, I'd fallen to letting the chef do their job.

"Eat up, baby."

"Mommy, can Pepper eat with me?"

"Pepper is eating her breakfast in the sunroom, love. You know Chef doesn't like puppies in the dining room." Yes, with the reassertion of her title, our chef was wielding her full power. "After you finish, we'll take her for a walk together."

"Okay," he said easy enough.

I bumped into Ryder walking out. He tucked his phone back in his pocket.

"I just hung up with Marcus," he said. "They're on the way from the airport and caught up with their messages. I told them we'd talk about what's going on in person."

My chest squeezed. "We have to do it now, Ryder. They need to know Maverick..." I trailed off.

They need to know Maverick's gone, but he will be safe at home soon. I refused to entertain another thought.

"Ezra can take Adam to school," Ryder said, taking my hand. "They'll be home in half an hour. We'll go after we eat."

I nodded. "What about your first class?"

"I'll be late."

We kissed, then I went upstairs to finish getting ready. Adam was done and leash in hand when I came down. Chuckling, I hugged the stuffing out of my cutie. He missed his dad like crazy, but Adam was incapable of losing his sweet smile for good.

After Pepper's walk, I sent Adam to school with Ezra and slid in Ryder's car. I still said we didn't need to have more cars than there were people in the house, but the boys laughed every time.

I traced the leather trim. *I wonder if I'll ever feel like this is my world.*

"What are you thinking?" Ryder asked. He started the car and drove for the gates.

"I still feel like a Wakefield transplant most days," I said. "Cooking my own meals. Refusing to get a car. Price checking items in the store. It still hasn't hit me that this is my life now."

"Get used to it, Moon. You're not going anywhere. You're stuck with us."

I rolled my eyes. "Very sensitive, insightful talk, baby. All of my worries have poof—gone away."

Ryder chuckled. "You feel like this because you don't have a part of Evergreen that's your own yet. We're living in my family's mansion. We don't have dance classes or studios nearby. You don't even have your own room. How can it feel like home, Val? You haven't let yourself have a place in it."

I was quiet for a long time.

I wanted a sensitive, insightful comment, and Ryder gave me one. "You're right," I said softly. "I haven't taken a piece of our home for myself even though..."

"Even though what?" Ryder pressed.

I hesitated. "Even though I've imagined turning one of the downstairs guest rooms into a dance studio like you said. I don't need my own room, but it would be nice to have a place to dance around and be silly with Adam like we used to do."

"I'm an ass for not bringing this up sooner, Val. Any part of the house you want is yours. Anything you want is yours." He placed his hand over mine. "I'll clear out the guest room today."

I brought him to my lips, kissing his knuckles. "If you were an ass, that offer would've put everything right. But you're not. It's my fault for tiptoeing around like a guest. When Maverick's home, we'll do the Val's dance studio/office renovation together. I'm picturing you guys in tool belts and it's getting me hot."

Ryder jerked the wheel. "How hot, because I can pull over right now?"

"Behave."

We didn't pull over of course. We kept driving to deliver the worst news parents could hear.

The Beaumonts' butler opened the door as we hit the top step. Not a surprise. We had to be buzzed in through the gate. He knew we were coming.

"Good morning, Mr. Shea. Miss Moon. I trust you are well."

"Hello, Mr. Gillespie," I replied. "Did you take a vacation too?"

He bowed his head. Gillespie was a stout, serious man who suffered not a strand out of place. Seriously, his salt-and-pepper hair was gelled into submission, and his suit didn't dare wrinkle.

"Mr. and Mrs. Beaumont generously allowed me two weeks to visit family in Montana."

"I hope you had a great time. Family is important," I said. "Family is everything."

"Yes. This way to the drawing room."

So ended the longest conversation I had with the butler. If I was hoping he'd draw it out to postpone the conversation I really needed to have...

"Val. Ryder."

...it didn't work.

The drawing room was cozier than the name suggested. Instead of stuffy antique chairs and suits of armor, they opted for squashy couches, reclining armchairs, and no drapes on the big window that flooded the cream, airy space with light.

The Beaumonts rose from their armchairs and embraced us like their own children. In Ryder's case, they practically saw him as one. And I was quickly becoming the daughter-in-law.

"Sit. Relax," Marcus said. "Would you like some tea? We just called down to the chef for a pot of oolong."

The couple abandoned the armchairs for a loveseat together. Marcus draped his hand over his wife's shoulder, pressing a kiss to her temple. I loved seeing them together. After thirty years, a tech empire, three kids, and many pets, they still looked at each other like teenagers on their first date.

That's how the five of us will be in thirty years. There wasn't a doubt in my mind.

"No, thank you," I said. Reaching for Ryder, I squeezed his fingers. "We came because we need to tell you something and we had to do it in person."

Marcus scrunched his forehead. "This sounds very serious."

"It is serious," Ryder said. "We couldn't reach you or we would've told you right away."

"What's going on?"

"Maverick's been kidnapped," I said.

"Kidnapped?" they repeated, sharing a frown.

"After the tournament, I went to pick him up but he wasn't there. A teammate said they last saw him talking to a guy from my brother fraternity, Sawyer." My throat threatened to close. "Sawyer's gone too. I haven't been able to track him down either."

"Sawyer?" Marcus's frown deepened. "The boy Ezra said was kidnapped from the university?"

"He was, but it seems he's working for his kidnappers now," I said. "Ryder and I have gone to the police. They're doing everything they can, but it's not much." I leaned forward in my seat. "I'm so sorry I let this happen. If I had kept Maverick out of this whole mess, he'd be here with us now."

"Valentina."

"I don't know what the Sams want with him, but I don't believe they'll hurt him."

"Valentina," Marcus said. "If this is a joke, it's not funny."

"It's not a joke," Ryder said. "Maverick has been missing for weeks."

"He's not missing," his mom spoke up. "He needed time off."

"I know this is hard," I began, "but he really has been taken like Sawyer, Teagan, and others before him. I will find out where he is and bring him home."

"You're serious. You believe someone has taken Maverick," Marcus said, exchanging more looks with his wife. "Valentina, he is not missing. He hasn't been taken by this Sawyer or anyone else. Maverick needed a break from the stress of school and activities, so he took some time off for a bit."

"He didn't—"

Ryder touched my arm, silently staying me. "Why do you say that?" he asked.

"Because before we got your messages, we got Maverick's telling us what we told you." Marcus shook his head. "I can't believe he didn't tell you all of this. Just taking off without a word? No wonder you called the police."

I seized on his first sentence. "Message? You got a message from Maverick?"

"Yes," said his mom. "He's perfectly safe, Valentina. I'm so sorry you worried."

Now it was Ryder's turn to lean half off his seat. He stared at the couple with burning intensity. "Will you play it for us?"

"Certainly," said his father. Marcus fished the phone out of his pocket.

I stopped breathing as he tapped the screen. *Wait. What is happening?*

He set the cell on the coffee table between us. "Hey, Dad."

I shot up, snatching the phone. I gaped at Maverick's voice pouring out the speakers.

"I called to let you know I'm taking off for a while. Don't worry, I cleared it so I can take finals online. Everything's piling up on me and I need a break. I'll call you when I'm back. Bye."

The call ended, leaving a thick, pressing silence.

That was Maverick. I knew his voice better than my own. It was him as surely as my hands were shaking and the Beaumonts were looking at me strangely.

"Valentina? Are you okay?" Marcus asked.

"This isn't right," I rasped.

"Val, you heard the message. He's fine. He—"

"He just took off in the middle of the night with no car, and left me and Adam alone in a parking lot? He wouldn't do that, Marcus. No one would do that! They made him leave you that voicemail because Aiden isn't afraid of me, but he is afraid of you."

Marcus threw up his hands. "Valentina, hold on. I agree it's out of character for Maverick to take off like this, but if he is under stress, he may not be thinking clearly. Either way, my son wasn't forced to leave that message. We would know if he was."

"How?" I asked.

"Maverick is an intelligent young man. Smart enough to give a clue if he was being held against his will."

My reply was immediate. "Aiden Connelly is an intelligent young man too. The easiest thing to do is write the script and make Maverick read it word for word. No hidden clues added."

His mom clutched her husband's arm. "Maverick is fine, Val. He can't be— He just can't!"

"I know this is hard to hear, but this is real. That message is a lie. Maverick disappeared that night and I haven't heard from him since. You don't want to believe it, but all you have to ask yourself is if any amount of stress would make Maverick leave us the way he did." I clutched his phone in a strangling grip. "Adam asks for him every night."

The couple shared another look, and this time I didn't need to guess at what they were thinking.

"Phone," Marcus barked. He grabbed the cell and marched off, rattling off orders before he left the room.

"Valentina, start from the beginning. Who would take him and how close are the police to finding him?"

I relayed the entire story from the first day of orientation to the lack of progress the police and Ryder's security team were making. We both ended up missing our morning classes.

Ryder drove us to school. I couldn't begin to guess what was on his mind.

"I won't need a ride home today," I spoke up. "After classes, I'm going to the Sally house."

If I expected a reaction, I didn't get one. Ryder slid into the left lane, moving only to check his mirrors.

"I can't stay away from the people involved in this. Someone in that house knows more than they are saying, and I'm going to find out what."

"How?"

"I—"

"You've asked nicely," he continued. "That didn't work. You've dug into their pasts. That didn't work either. What are we doing differently this time, Valentina? Because they're not afraid of us, and they couldn't have made that clearer."

Surprisingly, I was ready for the blunt question. "How do you pry anything open, Ryder? Leverage."

"Don't leave me out."

I blinked at him. I was expecting a speech on it being too dangerous. Leave the dirty work to his security and stay away from the Sallys on top of it.

How long have you been with this man? He knows you better than that.

"I won't. We'll get him back. Together."

Ryder parked in the lot nearest my advanced dance composition class. We kissed on the sidewalk and went in opposite directions.

I couldn't focus in class. Instructor Everett called me out three times for messing up easy steps and bumping into people. She told me to take a break. After class, I had an hour to grab food with Sofia. She waved me over to her table in the back already loaded down with tacos.

"Thanks, Sof, I'm starved." I had a mouthful of carne asada by the end of the sentence.

"No problem. I'm glad you had time. I can fill you in on everything that's gone on in the house."

"Has Jade completely taken over?"

She snorted. "Not completely. We're still allowed to choose the film on movie nights." Sofia took a bite of taco, chewed, swallowed, and dabbed the corners of her mouth like the well-bred aristocrat she was. "She moved in quick while you were gone, Val. Undoing all the changes you made and setting a strict Leighton-style regime."

"What about Blair?"

"Blair gets in a clenched-jaw, backhandedly polite argument with her every other day. There's a battle over who outranks whom, and

Jade's asserting herself in the struggle, claiming she's doing everything by the book, so Blair doesn't have a valid reason to contradict her." Sofia gave me a look. "We need you."

"Good thing I'm coming back. There's going to be some changes to the way we do things, and if our housemother doesn't like it, she can get used to clenching her jaw on the sidelines. I'm done with these batshit rules and the ulterior motives for making us follow them."

"I've got your back."

"I know you do. That's why I need you to do something for me."

"Anything," Sofia said without skipping a beat. "Name it."

"All that research we did on past pledge classes," I said. "I need you to dig a few people up."

"VALENTINA!"

Palmer practically jumped in my arms. We hugged like we hadn't seen each other in years instead of a few weeks.

"How are you doing?" she asked. "Are the police closer to finding your boyfriend?"

"Not that they've told us," I said. "But I will find him. Nothing is going to stop me."

"You're so strong." She let me go, leading the way into the living room.

The news of my return must've spread for the coffee table was covered with treats. Cake pops, chips, cookies, candy, and fizzy drinks. Around the table were Mai, Keily, Carmen, and half a dozen sisters.

"Is this for me?"

"Of course it is. Sofia said you were coming back today, and carrot sticks and veggie smoothies are no way to celebrate." She grimaced.

"Been hitting the healthy food hard, haven't you?"

"You have no idea."

"Well, I've returned to save the day. And break the diets." I threw my arms out. "Bring it in."

They rushed me—piling on the hugs, warm greetings, and wishes for Maverick to return safe and sound.

"Valentina."

I stiffened.

"Welcome back. It's good to see you." Jade stepped into view.

They say eyes are the window into the soul. They're wrong.

Eyes are nothing but colored orbs spinning around in your skull. It's the curve of your lips. Twitch in your brow. Rigid set of your jaw. They will tell you everything you need to know as long as you're paying attention. For all that her eyes were shining and a smile flashed both rows of teeth, Jade was telling me she was not happy to see me.

Not by any stretch of the imagination.

"Good to see you too, Jade. Thanks for holding down the fort while I've been out."

"It's no problem. That's why I'm here."

The sisters broke away, helping themselves to food and claiming spots to sit and talk. It was me and Jade facing each other across the divide.

"Are you sure you're ready to come back?" she asked, smile in place. "You were struggling after Mason's disappearance and it began to affect your duties. Don't rush back if you're not ready."

"His name is Maverick," I corrected. "Don't pretend you don't know that when you and your buddies took him in the first place."

Jade's lips turned down as quickly as the volume. The sisters stared at us—cake pops half in their mouths.

"This is what I'm referring to," Jade said tightly. "These wild accusations have to stop, Valentina. I barely knew your boyfriend. Why would I kidnap him?"

I advanced on her. "That's a great question, and it's one I intend to discover when I expose you and the whole operation the Sams and

Sallys have been running over the years. You took the wrong one," I hissed. "That was your last mistake."

"I have no idea what you're talking about. You sound crazy," she snapped. "I was right, you're not ready to return to the Sally house. Go, Valentina. You can come back when you've cleared your head."

Grinning, I threw my hands out. "My head is clear, Jade. I know exactly what I want and what I will do. Every day Maverick's been away from me has solidified that. I will get him back," I said, "and until I do, I'll be here making sure none of my sisters disappear on a keg run."

Jade's eyes blazed. Maybe I was wrong. I was picking up something in those boiling pools, and it was not nice.

"They are not in danger. No one in this house is. You're spinning a web of delusions to help you face that your boyfriend is gone and you don't know why or how to get him back. Well, have you considered the son of a tech mogul like Marcus Beaumont would have more dangers following him than most? Anyone could have taken him to get to his father," Jade said. "But one thing I do know for sure is neither Zeta Rho nor Nu Alpha had anything to do with it."

I hummed. "Maverick gets involved with Aiden and Sawyer, and then disappears the same way Sawyer did... but assuming they're involved is a delusion? Play your games with someone else, Jade. I see through you."

"Hey, guys," Mai spoke up. "Maybe we should cool it. It's supposed to be a party."

"The party is over," Jade said. "Valentina is not ready to resume her duties. She's leaving."

"Actually, I'm not." I tore a bite off a brownie. "My time off was voluntary. You didn't have the power to make me leave then and you don't now. I checked.

"For me to be removed, you'd need two-thirds of the sisters to vote me out in a meeting Blair would have to call. You seem to be forgetting your duties as housemother, and they are not to undermine me, make changes behind my back, or order me out of the house like you're my actual mother." I squared her down. "You're overstepping, Jade. I think you should leave."

Jade started like I slapped her. "Excuse me?"

"Leave, Jade. This is a party with my friends and sisters, and the last thing I should have to deal with is being lied to and called crazy by a woman who knows more than she's saying. Get out."

Sofia got to her feet. "Go, Jade."

"Yeah," said Keily. "I don't know if Val's right, but I do know something's wrong with Aiden and what he gets up to in his basement. We've all got reason to feel uncomfortable about the way Zeta Rho and Nu Alpha treats us. At least Val tries to make this house a sisterhood."

"Agreed." Blair stepped in the room. "Val's an excellent president who is going through a hard time. Instead of calling her crazy in response to reasonable suspicion she has for people who investigated, hacked, and spied on us. Why don't you offer proof the fraternities are innocent? Until then, it's a party for the sisters. You're not invited."

Jade's mouth disappeared in a thin line.

I didn't know how she would respond. *I* didn't know how to respond. I appreciated and cared for my sisters, but I never expected them to have my back through this—besides Sofia. They haven't seen what I've seen, or unearthed the secrets I did. As far as they knew, this was a strict sorority with harsh requirements for getting in. Nothing more.

So, maybe they just trust me.

"I see," Jade said, tone blank. "I don't wish to cause any problems or upset anyone. My use of the word crazy was wrong. Valentina is going through a hard time and I could stand to be more compassionate." She met my eyes. "Valentina, I apologize. I truly wish your boyfriend returns safe and sound, and if there is anything I can do to help, please let me know. But I must make one thing clear—"

"No, you don't," I sliced in. "You've said all you need to say. Go."

Stiff backed, Jade walked out, head high. I waited till her door closed upstairs to speak.

"Ladies, if I haven't told you I love you a thousand times, let this be the first. The next nine hundred and ninety-nine are coming."

Blair pulled me down on the couch. Sofia closed the doors.

"Do you really think someone in Nu Alpha took your boyfriend?" Palmer asked. "Why?"

"Look, guys, I know this all seems hard to believe, and I don't want to scare anyone. But there was something wrong about the way Teagan and Sawyer left." I could say that since Teagan wasn't in the room. Though, I wished she was here to offer an explanation. A real one.

"When Ezra pushed it, Aiden threatened him. He told him to back off or he'd expose his secret and put his brother's life in danger."

Palmer gasped. "He what? So much for our secrets never being mentioned again."

"A promise that's likely been broken whenever a brother or sister got out of line. Aiden sure didn't hesitate." I took a deep breath. "After that, I didn't trust a thing Aiden said. Including that Sawyer was safe and sound wherever he sent him. When Sawyer and Teagan showed up claiming stints in rehab and time off for grieving, Maverick got close to Aiden and his buddies to find out the truth. On the night Maverick disappeared, he was seen talking to Sawyer."

I swept over them, meeting their eyes in turn. "You tell me if that's just a coincidence, and I should be looking at corporate enemies instead of the guy next door?"

A shudder went through Blair. "No, Val. If all that's true, Aiden's the only one I'd be looking at too."

"But how do you know it's connected to the entire fraternity and not just Aiden?" Keily whispered.

Leighton floated through my head. "Because people have been vanishing from these houses long before any one of us set foot on campus. There's something going on and my boyfriend is caught in the middle."

"What can we do to help?" Palmer asked.

"If you see or hear anything out of place, tell me. I haven't had a shred of proof to convince the police to take this more seriously. We have our own people searching for him, but they don't know where to start." My gaze drifted toward the ceiling. "I need someone to slip up. To say the wrong thing that leads to the right place."

"As in, you need us to break Jade," Blair said, dropping the sentence without inflection. "We get it."

"Do you?" I asked. "So, why are you willing to do it?"

"You're not the only one picking up on the bad smell around here, Val," Mai said. "Jade got rid of all the changes you guys made while you were gone. Even the ones Kessler approved. We were back to five-mile runs, jumping jacks, and silent study sessions masquerading as bonding time. For some reason, it's more important that we're buff automatons than it is for us to hit our goals and enjoy life in Zeta while we do it."

Palmer nodded along. "We couldn't help but ask why she's so rigid. What does the chapter truly want from us? They've taken things too far from the beginning, and we're starting to think there's a reason."

"There is a reason you all made it into Zeta Rho. It's because you're smart, strong women who see through bullshit. And that's why we're going to find out what the hell's going on around here."

We talked a bit more and then dropped the conversation to enjoy the party. I appreciated all those who spoke up for me, but it wasn't everyone in the room. More than a few of the sisters just sat there eating their cake pops and nodding in the right places. What was truly going on in their mind, I couldn't guess.

I had no intention of letting everyone know how far I was willing to go to save Maverick. Let them think I was waiting around for someone to slip up. Underestimating me is exactly why they would.

After the food was consumed and we were high on sugar, I helped clean up and move the furniture out of the way. We piled on the floor with blankets and pillows to watch a cheesy rom-com I forgot the name of the minute Ryder started texting me.

Ryder: Where are you? This is around the time I fulfill my duties to cheer you up. I take my responsibilities seriously.

A smile played at my lips. This was around the time Ryder was undressing me, but he did that every day and pretty much whenever we were alone.

Valentina: Oh? And what would we be doing if I was there and you were on duty.

Ryder: I'd lick the goose bumps off your skin, reducing you to melted bones in our bed. I'd wrap those legs around my head and taste every drop of juice from your pussy. Once I've got you purring, I'd flip you over and pound you into the headboard. You'd have a laurel imprint on your face for days.

"Wow," Mai said. She openly read the screen over my face. "The man knows how to evoke imagery."

I scrabbled away, ducking into a corner to hide my red face and explicit texts.

Valentina: All very tempting, my love, and I will be taking you up on that. But I don't need cheering up today. I've cycled out of crushingly depressed and moved on to angry. Very, very angry. I cussed out Jade. A move I think she's going to make me regret.

Ryder: How? By threatening you the way they threatened Ezra. They don't have proof to back up what Lewis wrote on that paper. Considering I'll make sure it's the last thing she ever does, your housemother isn't going to waste a good intimidation on that.

Another text beeped my phone.

Ryder: Unless you've got another reason for trying to provoke her. Are you hoping you'll be the next one to disappear? If you poke hard enough, they might snatch you up and take you to Maverick.

I shut off the phone, holding it against my chest. Loving men who knew me so well wasn't always a gift.

It beeped again. I forced myself to look at the message.

Ryder: Don't try it. If your stubbornness doesn't give a shit what I say, then think about Adam. He can't handle his mom vanishing on him.

My heart thumped hard in my rib cage.

Valentina: That's low bringing Adam into this. The last thing I want is our son confused and scared. That's why I have to bring his father home. Today I had to tell the Beaumonts that not only is Maverick missing, but some twisted kidnapper is sending fake messages and fucking with them. That was the last straw.

Valentina: I've been waiting weeks for Jacob or the cops to give me news they're close to finding him. Now I'm taking matters into my own hands.

Ryder: There are so many things wrong with your plan, Val, I don't know where to start. Whoever these people are, they keep psychos like Leighton Lewis around. Instead of picking you up and taking you to Maverick, they might kill you! Val, do not give that woman any reason to think you're a threat. Promise me.

I dropped the phone on my lap and clutched my head. Everyone was focused on the movie. They didn't see me in the corner, falling apart.

Was Ryder right?

Of course he was. I didn't underestimate the people who employed Aiden Connelly and were on Leighton Lewis's speed dial. I knew they had to be dangerous, and that's why every day Maverick was in their hands tore me to shreds.

I know him. I know Maverick is fighting as hard to get back to me as I am to get to him. If I'm not willing to risk my life to save him, then what have the years we've been together meant?

My phone went off. Ryder was done with texting.

I took it out of the room to answer.

"Ryder."

"Val, promise me."

"I promise I won't be reckless." I ventured farther down the hall, peeking Jade in the kitchen.

She stood with her back to me, chopping vegetables on the block. Jade must have heard me but she didn't turn around.

"How will you keep that promise when you're trying to provoke them? We don't know why they took Maverick in the first place. We don't know how they got him to leave that voicemail. We don't know anything. Now's the time to get Jade to *talk*, not force her to act."

I continued up to Sofia's room. "I have an idea for that."

"Care to share?"

"At home. I will promise you this," I said. "I'll give plan A a try before resorting to plan B. But I'm not sitting on my ass anymore."

"And such a fine ass it is."

"Ryder."

"I get it, Val. Don't you think I feel the same? But what if I told you I was walking around Greek Row with a 'kidnap me' sticker on my forehead? Would you be cool if I was the next one to go missing?"

"Of course not."

"Why not? They might take me to Maverick."

"You've made your point," I gritted. "I said I'd start with talking."

A thought occurred to me.

"And I know exactly who we need to talk to."

RYDER

"Come home," I said.

"I'll be there in an hour. Let Adam stay up so I can snuggle him to bed. Love you."

"Love you too."

I ended the call. Leaning back in my chair, Cara opened her eyes to give me a reproachful look. I was her cat bed for the evening, and her cat bed didn't move.

I scratched the over-pampered puss under the chin and she purred to rumble the house. All was forgiven.

"Ryder, darling." Mom came in and kissed my cheek. "I gave up waiting and came looking for you. It's time for dinner."

"I was calling to see where Valentina was. She'll be late. I'll tell Chef to keep my food warm so we can eat together."

"That's fine." Her gaze scanned the large, shadowed room.

Benjamin Shea's old office was a floor down and gutted from the grand, stately room and turned into Cara's—complete with cat trees, toys, and her actual bed. Yes, we gave the cat a bedroom, and yes, we did so knowing Benjamin would hate it.

That left me to claim his old library as my office. There were no windows. Most of the books were moved to make way for the crates of company files, and two armchairs and a couch were pushed closer to the fireplace so my desk could fit inside. I could hear the thoughts going through her head before she voiced them.

"This office is so small and stuffy, sweetie. Why won't you move into the space in the east wing?"

"Because we all sleep in the west wing. I'm close by when Adam wants to wander in and pretend he's working on a big merger with his papers and crayons in front of the fireplace."

She laughed. "So adorable," she said, brimming with fondness.

If I wasn't fairly secure in her love for me, I'd think Adam beat me out for favorite. It wouldn't be a surprise if he did. He had a gift for melting the ice around the coldest hearts. For someone as warm and caring as Mom, she didn't stand a chance.

"How are you feeling?"

Mom dropped her chin, giving me a look. "I feel just fine. I would tell my doctor if I felt otherwise."

I put my hands up in surrender. "I wasn't worrying. I was asking like a good son. I could not give a crap about your health if that makes it better?"

That got me another look. I couldn't win.

"How are you doing, love?" She tugged my earlobe the way she used to do when I was a kid. "We haven't really sat down and talked about how you're handling Maverick's disappearance. I used to say you got tired of waiting for me to give you siblings, so you when out and found your own. I know this is hard for you. You don't have to put on a brave face."

My fists balled under the table. Cara meowed for me to continue her stroking. Mom picked her up and sent her off to find food.

"I'm not putting on a brave face, Mom. I'm not hiding how I think about this situation. There are secrets in that fraternity that someone or someones are willing to do anything to protect, and we were the idiots that thought we could handle it alone. Maverick paid the price."

"We don't know that, son. Marcus called me today and said he left them a voicemail expressing the stress was getting to him. There are other explanations than taken by a shadow organization."

"Maybe, but up and running out on Val isn't one of them."

She nodded slowly. "So, you truly believe someone connected to this... Nu Alpha Theta has taken Maverick like they have others? And the whole time this has been going on under everyone's nose?" Mom took my hand. "You must be terrified for Valentina being in the middle of this. Not to mention what Maverick is going through right now.

"Ryder, this is beyond you, me, Jacob, or the three-officer police team down at Evergreen PD. We need to get the dean involved. The FBI as well."

"I considered that, Mom, but they're covering their tracks and they're doing it well." I fixed on the fire, wondering if it was half as hot as the rage biting at my soul. "Valentina thought she had them—whoever them is—when she looked up the people who've gone missing from the sorority over the years. Then they showed up at the fundraiser.

"She knows something is happening to these people, but when Kainer and Burn are smiling their way through and backing up the fake story, Val looks like the one with the problem." Holding back a frustrated noise, I pushed back my chair. "Let's change the subject. I've gone around and around this many times, and I'm no closer to making sense of what's going on in that house. For now, I will have dinner with you, Mom. Chef said she made my favorite."

Mom hooked through my elbow. "She did. Lamb cutlets, glazed carrots, and roasted potatoes. I was afraid she'd leave us when our family grew, and all these differing palates changed up the menu. Instead, she's loving the challenge. Tomorrow, we're having banana pancakes and cinnamon oatmeal. Adam's favorite breakfast."

"Have you noticed Adam's favorites top the menu most days out of the week? The kid stole her love too."

Mom laughed. "It's what he does."

I observed her out of the corner of my eye. Mom loved having little feet running through the mansion again. She didn't push it, but I knew she was counting the days till we welcomed another little one with Valentina.

Mom wanted more kids. She might have had them if she wasn't trapped in a marriage with a sociopath. In the end, there was only me fathered by a man I didn't know.

I passed downstairs, heading for the dining room.

Countless times it was on the tip of my tongue to ask her. *Who is my real father?*

Every time I bit the question off and swallowed it. I couldn't let her know Valentina betrayed her confidence. That would make the conversation about how I found out instead of the fact she didn't tell me herself. Something I tried not to be angry about. Most days I succeeded.

No one on this planet should go a day believing they were related to Benjamin Shea.

"Mom, can I ask you something?"

In the dining room, I held out her chair at the head of the table and claimed the one next to her. The first course was warm on our plates.

"Anything, dear."

"Will you tell me the truth this time?"

She paused reaching for her napkin. A slight hesitation I would've missed if I wasn't paying attention.

"I always tell you the truth, Ryder."

"Why did you marry Benjamin?"

Mom sighed. With a breath, the life and color went out of her. Partly why she avoided the question, and I stopped asking it years ago.

But that day—the day my brother was missing and my girlfriend was risking her life over hidden secrets—I needed someone to tell me the truth.

"Ryder, we've been through this."

"You said you were under pressure to make a good match and you chose Benjamin because he put on a good show of a decent human being. But why were you under pressure, Mom? Why him?"

"Why is this so important to you, Ryder?"

"Because that man changed the course of our lives forever. Is it wrong for me to want to understand how we got here?"

The lines around her eyes softened. "No, son. It's the most natural thing in the world. Wanting to know our beginning."

I waited—eating a few bites while she collected herself.

"My parents owned a restaurant chain, as you know," she began. "Our entire family relied on it. Uncles, aunts, cousins. They worked in the restaurant or contributed to it in some way. When business took a turn, it wasn't just our ruin my parents were facing. It was the domino that would topple everyone relying on them. They couldn't let that happen."

Mom stopped again. I didn't rush her.

"When I got into Evergreen, my parents didn't outright say it, but their excitement at the wealthy prospects the school would give me was obvious. At least they didn't say it at first. As the years went on, old guy friends from school were invited over for dinner all too often. I came home from university to a surprise dinner guest almost every week.

"Most nights, it was Benjamin. I can't say when we started dating," she confessed. "One day, we were a couple and I wasn't there when it happened."

"Did you play the part for your parents' sake?"

"For them and mine," she replied. "At the time, I was with a kind, wonderful guy who went to Somerset on scholarship. My parents would never have approved, but for once, I loved having something that was all mine."

I sat up straighter in my seat. "Who was the guy?"

"Doesn't matter," Mom said, shaking her head. "Because at the end of my senior year, our restaurants were closing one after the other. My father's application for a loan was denied, and Benjamin proposed to me. It sunk in that our last hope to save my family was me. So I said yes."

Mom laid her hand over mine. "I wish I had a better explanation for you, Ryder. In the end, it's the same old story. I married the beast for money."

"You didn't marry him for money. You married him for family." I tried to keep the question down. It forced its way back up. "What happened to your boyfriend? The wonderful guy."

She smiled—a quick quirk of the lips that was gone as quickly as it happened. "He understood why we had to end the relationship. We stayed friends for a while after graduation, but eventually he got a job out of state and we lost contact. I believe he's married with children now."

My father? My half-siblings? Am I getting the first mention of them? I laid my head on our clasped hands. *Will you ever tell me?*

"You're so brave, Mom."

"Oh, love." She stroked my hair. "You don't have to say that."

"I mean it. I have everything to learn from you to become even half as selfless and a fraction as patient."

"Don't make me cry," she said, voice trembling.

I raised my head, returning to my meal. "Then, I'll make you laugh. I caught Cara riding Pepper's back this morning like a sultan. The girl officially has everyone in the house at her beck and call."

Mom's laugh rang out as expected. "Poor puppy. She had to accept her fate eventually."

Mom and I stayed in the dining room long after we cleared the first, second, and dessert course. Long enough Val returned and joined us.

"How was your first day back at the sorority?" Mom asked.

"Eventful." Val held my hand under the table. "I know all the reasons I chose to join and become president of the sorority, but I can't help thinking how different things would be if I kept walking past the Zeta booth that day at orientation."

"We all have those thoughts," Mom said. I imagined she was thinking of a certain beast who kept coming to dinner. "But even among the bad, you find good you wouldn't trade anything for. We will bring Maverick home, Valentina. I have no doubt."

"You've never lied to me before, Caroline," Val replied, voice soft. "So, I guess I have to believe you."

"You do." Mom pushed back from the table. "I'm going to get ready for bed. Come up and talk to me before you go to sleep."

"I will," said Val.

A talk I wasn't invited to. Their relationship used to bother me back when I thought it was built on guilt and a sense of obligation. I didn't want my mother to feel she had to pay for Benjamin's sins. That was my job. To support Valentina. To give her everything she needed, and make up for the seed of hatred I let Benjamin plant in me.

That was how I used to feel. Now I could see their friendship was genuine. Two mothers, raising sons through hardship. In a lot of ways, they've helped each other more than anyone could.

"What are you thinking about?" Val asked. She brushed her lips along the shell of my ear.

"I was thinking you like my mother more than me."

Chuckling, she nipped my earlobe. "Ridiculous. I love you both the same."

"Damn. I don't even win out for delivering daily orgasms?"

"I've got lots of guys on that."

"That's it!"

Val took off shrieking. I chased her through the hall, over the living room couch, and past a barking Pepper. Valentina shot for the back door and escaped outside.

I scooped her up and tipped us both in the pool.

"Ryder!"

"I've got you." I secured her legs around me, wading deeper till the water reached our chin.

Thick, chestnut strands stuck to her cheeks. I brushed them back, lingering on her lips on the way down. Droplets clung to long lashes. They fell as she blinked—dripping on my fingers.

Valentina Moon was truly the most beautiful creature to walk this earth. She didn't believe it. She didn't notice the people who stopped in their tracks as she walked by. The men who looked at me with envy or the women who blinked twice to see if she was real. It amazed me every day that she chose me. But if I was honest, I never planned to give her a choice.

"You're mine, Moon. You know that, don't you?"

"It has been mentioned once or twice."

"You don't have to say it. You already know you have my balls in a vise."

She giggled. "If that's your way of saying I know you love and are devoted to me, then yes. I have your balls right where I want them."

We kissed—slow and thorough, tightening said balls in my pants. A normal reaction. I got hard every time I kissed Val. Extremely inconvenient in public.

"I've been thinking," I said against her lips.

Val teased the hairs at the nape of my neck. "About what?"

"About fathers. Mine in particular."

She stilled. "You mean your biological father?"

I nodded. "I've downplayed how much I need this, Val. To myself too. I've tried to believe it doesn't matter, but I need to know. I can't tell you how many times I've watched Jacob toss a water bottle and thought *all I have to do is send it out for DNA.*"

"Ryder." She kissed the tip of my nose. "I know it's hard. Whatever you want to do, I support you. Tell Caroline that you know. She's probably waiting for the day you do. This is a big secret to keep from the man I love."

"She hasn't asked you to?"

"No." Val grabbed a passing float and climbed on. I swam her around the pool, enjoying her hands tangled in my hair. "We haven't spoken about that day in years, Ryder."

"Even so, I'm not going to tell her how I found out. I'll say I found the will or something like that when the time comes. For now, I'd like to find him on my own. Mom's been through enough. I don't want to drag up any more painful memories."

"I'll help however I can, if help is what you want." She grinned at me. "But I think you can skip fishing Jacob's bottles out of the trash. You look nothing like that man."

"Genetics are weird, Moon. I could've inherited silver eyes from way up his family tree."

She gazed up at the stars. "How strange would that be if he was near you the entire time? Protecting you."

"How strange would it be if it was the man she was supposed to have a future with? Kind and caring and given up for the man who was supposed to be her savior and instead became her nightmare."

"Are you speaking about someone in particular?"

I stopped her float at the foot of the stairs. "Let's go up. I'll have Chef warm your food and bring it to our room."

She grabbed hold of me. "Ryder, tell me."

"I don't know that there's anything to tell," I admitted. "Mom told me about a man she dated in college. She loved him. I could see that clear as day. She said he was around after she got married and didn't move away till sometime later. Mom got pregnant with me a year after marrying Benjamin."

"So, you're thinking if this great love was still in her life around the time you were conceived, maybe he..." Val trailed off.

She didn't have to say more. We were both thinking the same thing.

"Not as far-fetched as the bodyguard, right?"

I lifted her in my arms and carried her inside. Val kept her voice low though Mom couldn't hear us from her room.

"How will you find him without asking her?"

"There must be old photos lying around. If I can't dig up anything, I'll have the conversation, but it's easier for me to do it this way. I'm sure she has her reasons for hiding the truth. They may be the same reasons that push her to lie to me."

"Everything she's done is to protect you, Ryder," Val said. "I don't doubt that for a second." She buried her face in my neck. "Just tell me what you need me to do, and I'll do it."

"I will, but not now. We have to focus on finding Maverick. I've gone twenty-one years without knowing the guy. I can wait a few more weeks."

Upstairs, we washed off and I curled up in bed with her and her dinner. Val fed me bits of lamb in between telling me about the showdown in Zeta Rho.

"Both our jaws were on the floor when the sisters spoke up for me. I lowkey assumed they all thought I was paranoid. Overreacting to a few sisters dropping out of school."

I licked her fingers claiming my second dinner. "It's like your VP said. Everyone's still sore at having their secrets spilled to the entire room. I don't think you're the first to have suspicions, Val. You're just the first to act on it."

"That we know of. Other people might have spoken out and disappeared like the rest. But then they came back," she said under her breath. "Where were Sawyer and Teagan? What the fuck happened to them while they were gone? If this is all so innocent, why did Jade look at me like she wished the van sent to pick me up would run me over instead?"

"There is no van coming to pick you up. Do not provoke that woman if you vanishing will be the outcome. I'm serious, Val. If something happens to you, I will not be held responsible for my actions."

"I told you," she soothed, rubbing my chest. "Sofia and I are trying out other avenues first. Starting with Aiden."

"Finals are in two weeks. If he's wherever Maverick is, he'll have to come back for those. This is his last year."

"That's what I was thinking. It's no coincidence he's out sick the same time Maverick goes missing. The best way to get to him is through the man who knows where he is," she said. "But I'm not waiting for two weeks. For all we know, he'll arrange to take them online. Maverick's waited for us long enough." She kissed me. "Caroline's staying up for me. Get some sleep and I'll be back to spoon you later."

"I'm the big spoon. Just get naked and slip under me. All will be right with the world."

She tossed me a wink and headed out.

There were half a dozen things I needed to do for the company, and three assignments to complete for school. Val would walk back in here to me wide awake under a mountain of papers.

A knock sounded at the door. "Daddy?"

"Come in, Adam."

The little boy vaulted onto the mattress, scattering my papers.

"Where's Mommy?"

"She's with Cara," I said. "Want to go find her?"

"No." He burrowed into my side, laying his head on my chest. "Are we working?"

I chuckled. "I'm working. You're avoiding bedtime." I pointed at the screen. "See this? It's the list of health plans I have to choose from for our employees."

"What's a health plan?"

I tried to explain as best as I could.

"Can I pick?"

"Sure."

I made no secret that when Adam was of age, the company would be his if he wanted it. It was important to both me and Valentina that he knew he had a choice. So far, he was taking his role of future CEO very seriously, and often thought he had to put everything down and "work" when he caught me in my office.

"This one cost more money, but will give more help," I said, keeping it simple. "This one costs less money and gives less help, but it has an extra plan for people hurting in here." I tapped this chest. "This one cost the least and gives very little help. What do you think?"

Adam screwed up his face, putting his six-year-old mind to the task.

"None of them," he announced.

"Why?"

"Because we need one that gives the most help and has an extra plan for people hurting inside."

"Ah, well, that would be this one." I scrolled down to the listing for Dempra HealthCare. "Pricey, but it covers almost everything we can think of."

"That one," Adam said confidently.

"Dempra it is." The one I was going to pick all along. "I'm glad I've got you to run these decisions by, Little Moon. We're going to make a good team."

"I'm not little anymore. I'm going to be seven." Adam threw out his hands. "I'm Big Moon!"

"Big Moon?" I repeated, rolling it around. "I like the sound of that."

"What else do we have to do?"

"We've got to read these reports. Wanna get Tim and your blanket, and help me get through these?"

"Okay."

Adam ran off to get his stuffed giraffe and matching blanket. If he didn't march back in ready to take over the corporate world, who did? Twenty minutes into my droning, the kid was out like a light.

His curly head dwarfed beneath my hands. I gazed down at him—the usual curious mix of feelings swirling in my head as I did.

I understood Benjamin Shea even less every time I looked at Adam. Filled with bitterness and hatred because the boy he raised wasn't his own. Anger over being lied to aside, his feelings toward my mother didn't have to sour his feelings toward me. He could've had a son. He could've loved the family he was given.

But for that to happen, you'd have to be capable of love in the first place.

The bastard was rotted straight to his core, and receiving the son he always wanted wouldn't have changed that.

Adam would never know that man. His name wouldn't be spoken in his presence. His portraits wouldn't loom over him. His legacy wouldn't stretch across his life. Most importantly, he wouldn't question if his fathers were there for him.

Benjamin Shea destroyed everything he touched. In his place, I would put the pieces back together.

"Oops. Looks like someone decided to join us." Val stood in the doorway. "Want me to bring him back to his bed?"

"He's fine. I've got to stay up a bit longer reading. He's filling in on cuddle duty."

She kissed me. "Don't stay up too late. Love you."

"Love you."

When Valentina was sound asleep, Adam snuggled under her chin, I opened the email Jacob sent while I was reading reports.

Everything they had on the people of Zeta Rho Sigma and Nu Alpha Theta. Almost a hundred files.

Yes, this was going to be a long night.

Chapter Three

*V*alentina

"Where are we going again?"

"It's a town called St. Germaine," I replied. "Caroline is wonderful letting us use the jet. She said it'll be fueled and ready to go by the time we get there."

It had been a long, tense week of classes, bonding activities, Zeta Rho, and Jade.

With me back in charge, I returned us to the new way of doing things, and Jade was not happy about it. She came to every exercise session with her timer, making sure the girls got their seventy-five minutes and calling out those who didn't. At night while we hung around in the kitchen talking and making dinner, she parked herself at the island with whatever she was working on—not a part of the conversation, but always close by.

It was a relief to reach the end of the week. Every day I wasn't actively looking for Maverick was a strip off my soul. I couldn't sit around waiting for him to walk through the door. I had to bring him home.

"What are you going to do, Val?" Jaxson had one eye on me and the other on the road. "We're past the point of *willing to do anything* to rescue Maverick, but we can't help him if our asses are in jail."

"We're not going to hurt anybody. I just want to ask"—I checked the names again—"Jolene and Robert Connelly a few questions."

"What's the theory? You think they know something they're not telling the police?" Jaxson turned onto the road that led to the airfield.

"Officer Mylow says he spoke to them and they don't know where their son is. They thought he was at school."

"Yes, I think they know more. If not about where he is, they know who he is. I want to look in their eyes when I ask if their son is a duplicitous liar who's hiding something and laughing at us about it. Let's see if they have the same skill for evading questions in person."

Jaxson bobbed his head. "Like I said, we're past the point of willing to do anything and in a new category of desperate. Whatever it takes."

"Thank you. I'm glad you're here." I rubbed his forearm. "Sofia was supposed to come, but we decided it's not a good idea to leave Jade alone right now. She doesn't like that control was wrestled away from her, and I want to know everything she does while I'm away."

"I'd like to know everyone she talks to," Jaxson said. "That stunt she pulled at the fundraiser, making all the vanished brothers and sisters reappear. She didn't do that alone."

"She can't have. She wasn't around when all this started."

"Exactly."

I took a deep breath and let it go. "I should say what I've been thinking for a while, Jaxson. There is a secret organization— A cult," I stated. "For select members of Nu Alpha and Zeta Rho, they're chosen based on some kind of criteria that sets them apart from the rest, and then they're taken to wherever they keep them until they decide to join."

"Why would they need to be taken somewhere else?" Jaxson asked. "It's risky. Sawyer's snatch and grab invited all kinds of problems. Leighton and Aiden were presidents. They controlled the house and what happened in it. Why couldn't they do their inducting there?"

I chewed over that for a minute. "Because if I think about the little I know of cults and how they work, an easier target is an isolated one. What if their pitch goes down better if there's no one around and no chance of escape?"

"Makes sense. Horrifying, but it makes sense. Still," he said.

"Still what?"

"This is obviously a secret they're determined to hide from the world and the rest of the brothers and sisters. You've got to think at least a few of the chosen have rejected their elevator pitch. Refused to join. What happens to them, Valentina?" He met my eyes at the red light. "Because no one's come back shouting about cults and brainwashing initiations."

I swallowed hard. Logan flashed through my mind. "I don't know what happens to the people who say no, Jaxson. I haven't let myself go there."

"Then, I'm not going there either. Let's just talk to this couple. See what they have to say for themselves."

"Thank you."

As promised, the jet was fueled and ready on the tarmac. The attendant helped me up the stairs and I settled on a comfy leather lounge beside a glass of wine and selection of shortbread cookies. This new life of mine would still take some getting used to.

I was talking to Caroline in her room that night about driving up five hours to see Aiden's family, and she said not to be silly and take the jet.

I laced my fingers through Jaxson's. I'd take him too.

Ezra and Ryder both had to work, and Adam had it in his head that when Daddy Ryder was busy, he's busy too. My music producer love had no such obligations of homework and studying for upcoming finals.

"How is everything going at the label?" I asked. "I'm sorry. I feel like we haven't really talked since—"

"My brother and your boyfriend was kidnapped," he finished. "We've both had a lot on our minds, baby. I don't blame you for being distracted."

"Still, I want to know what's going on with you. Tell me about work. Every band you've signed. Every song about to take over the airwaves. Every stalker lurking around the corner."

"Ha ha." Jaxson threw me a lopsided grin. "Glad we've gotten to the place we can laugh about it."

"We are a magnet for danger. Secret societies, stalkers, homicidal sorority presidents, cults, and disappearances. If I didn't learn to let it go and be light about it, it'd have crushed me a long time ago. But between you and me, I can't wait for the normal, boring lives everyone else gets where it's just the five of us and our many kids."

"By many, how much are we talking?"

"Only-child syndrome. I've always wanted a big family. When I picture the future, I see little ones with your smile, Ezra's eyes, Maverick's curls, and Ryder's raven hair." I winked at him. "We'll just keep going until all those traits are made real in our babies."

He blew out a breath. "Damn. So much for one more to give Adam a friend. But alright, big family it is." Jaxson smiled. "I caught that only-child syndrome too."

It was perfect little pockets of time like this. Talking about our future children. Watching Ryder read to Adam. Stealing kisses on the couch with Ezra. Those were the pockets of normal I felt stretching out through our lives. This was how perfect we would always be. The six of us.

With Maverick.

My gaze drifted out the window as we took off.

I will bring you home.

"WELCOME AND THANK YOU for staying with us at the Sunflower Inn. If you'd like to follow me, I'll show you to your room."

A tall, cheery lady stepped out from behind the checkout desk and motioned to the stairs. We planned to spend the weekend here in case the first conversation with the Connellys didn't go well and we had to go back for another.

"TripAdvisor said this is the best hotel in town," I offered.

"It's cute."

The Sunflower was cute. They leaned into their flower theme and covered the walls in bright, yellow wallpaper. The entire place had an old-timey charm that seeped through its pores and spread through the small town. As we drove through, we spotted neighbors talking to each other over the fence. Kids played hockey in the street and parted for our rideshare to go by. This was a world unlike our Evergreen.

The innkeeper dropped us off at a door labeled the "Orchid Room." We stepped inside to see it was just a cute name. Other than the single potted orchid by the bed, the room was tastefully done in mocha wallpaper that matched the dark brown satin sheets on the queen bed. A tiny corner breakfast nook claimed a spot next to the window. Jaxson and I could sit and gaze out at the creek flowing behind the inn.

"It's perfect," I said. "Thank you."

"Let me know if you need anything."

"We will."

She left us alone. Jaxson stripped me immediately and tossed me squealing on the bed. We fooled around, knocking the slippery pillows to the floor and nearly sliding down with them. After, we lay with the sweat cooling on our skin and blankets tangled at our legs.

"What's the place called?" Jaxson chased a bead of sweat running between my breasts with his finger.

"The Hometown Dive," I said. "It's small but popular. Apparently, Aiden's parents took it over from his grandfather. It's an institution around here."

"We'll want to catch them after the restaurant closes. We don't want them to use customers as a reason not to talk with us."

"Good idea." I rubbed suddenly shaky hands on my thighs. "Goodness, it feels like we're going into an interrogation. We came to ask a supposedly normal couple about their supposedly normal son, but nothing since I joined the sorority has been as it seemed. What will Aiden do when he finds out we were here?"

"He will find out." Jaxson kissed just below my cheekbone. "His parents have no reason not to tell him we were here. But if he's trying to keep up the supposedly normal routine, he wouldn't have a problem with us asking a few questions."

"Unless he's holding Maverick and knows the upper hand is his."

"Don't go there," Jaxson whispered. "We came here to find the answers that would lead us to Maverick. That's exactly what we're going to do."

I nodded. "I know we will."

"Distraction?"

"What do you have in mind?"

"We could play a game."

"I'm listening."

A devilish grin broke out on his lips. "You could time how many tongue fucks it takes for you to explode on my mouth."

My cheeks heated. "That sounds like my kind of game."

Twenty-two turned out to be the answer. We played that and many other games as we waited for the restaurant to near closing.

At eight o'clock, we dragged ourselves out of bed, showered, and left the inn. The town of St. Germaine was even lovelier draped in starlight. Felt like we were a couple after the perfect date, walking slowly hand in hand to draw out the final goodbye on the doorstep.

"Could we not get our hands on their home address?"

"I have it," I said. "Decided it would be less creepy to talk to them in the restaurant rather than show up on their porch. Less likely to have a door slammed in our face too."

"I'll let you handle the questioning. Follow your lead."

"If I'm honest, I'll be making it up as we go."

"Are we coming up with a story or going with honesty?"

Hometown Dive loomed at the end of the street.

"Both."

A few people idled outside the restaurant, getting in a last chat before they split for their cars. On a Friday night, there were a fair number of diners inside laughing, eating, and clinking beers. We stopped to take in the little place.

It was easy to see what made it so popular. The restaurant resembled a log cabin complete with a swinging wooden sign announcing its name. Big windows afforded the customers a view of the busy main street interaction and the lake beyond. On one side, the bar was filled with rowdy guys hollering at the television, which left the family side separated by a wall and door. Something for everyone.

We stepped inside to the host's greeting.

"Table for two, please," Jaxson said.

"Right this way."

We weaved around red upholstered booths to a small two-person in the back. She swept out a hand for me to sit. "Haven't seen you folks around here before. New to town?"

"Arrived today," I said. "Your town is a little slice of heaven. I can't get over how beautiful it is here."

She beamed. "That it is."

"The couple who owns it are actually the parents of a friend of mine. I was hoping to meet them."

"You know Aiden?"

"Very well," said Jaxson.

"Ah, how nice of you to drop in to meet them. I'm afraid Robert and Jolene aren't here."

My face fell. "They're not?"

She shook her head. "They're getting older, so they're beginning to leave the day-to-day running to the assistant manager."

"Oh, that's disappointing," I said as I took my seat. "At least I can tell Aiden I tried a few things off the menu."

Jaxson waited till she was gone to speak. "What now?"

"Now we move on to creepy. I have the address. We go tomorrow morning and find out the truth about Aiden Connelly."

"Hopefully we don't get the door slammed in our face." He curled his fingers through mine. "But if we do, at least we came out here and did something."

"Another thing we haven't talked about." I stroked the soft skin between his thumb and forefinger. "How are you doing with all this?"

"It may sound weird since they managed to pick him up and cart him off, but I know Maverick's okay. He was always the strongest of us, and I don't mean physically. He's always had this quiet center that grounded him while the world fell to shit around him. He's just too strong to be broken, Valentina."

Tears prickled behind my eyes. "I both needed to hear that and knew it at the same time. Maverick is strong inside and out. I know he's okay."

"Tomorrow we'll see his folks," Jaxson said. "Tonight, we're in a town you're clearly crushing on, with a delicious-looking menu and a warm bed. Take the night off from worry, Val. Everything's going to be fine."

I took a deep breath, held it, and released it slowly. Did it work to get rid of my worry? No. But at least for tonight, I could pause, breathe, and reconnect with my love. In the morning, I'd get what I came here for.

Jaxson ordered smothered pork chops while I helped myself to buffalo mac 'n' cheese with a side salad. We picked off each other's plates, groaning at the flavors popping and flirting on our tongue. This was the real reason the town loved this place. The food was incredible.

We finished up paying for our meal and took the long way back to the inn.

"Do you ever wish you grew up somewhere like this?" I asked. The streets were quiet this late at night. "Simple. Homey. Knowing your neighbors as well as you know your family."

"There's an appeal to living the small-town life. I can see it. But no, I wouldn't trade Evergreen for St. Germaine. It's not about the money," Jaxson said. "It's... As weird as it sounds, I kinda liked that Dad and I were in our own world. He was this great, important man and I had him all to myself.

"If I grew up in a place like this where everyone knows and likes each other, Dad probably would've felt more comfortable leaving me with the babysitter up the street. Or dropping me off at the after-school playgroup. I like that I grew up two steps behind him."

I rested my head on his arm. "I know what you mean. Wakefield was a rough place and Mom didn't feel comfortable leaving me with people either. It was tough circumstances, but I loved that I was always close to the one person who made me feel safe. I want our kids to feel that close to us. But I want them to have this too," I said, sweeping out my hand. "A community."

"We're talking a lot about kids today. Is there something you want to tell me?"

"No." I poked his side. "There is no baby in this belly. I've just been thinking about after Somerset. Is Evergreen it for us? Is this where we're building our home and family?"

"Do you want to be somewhere else?"

"No. It's not that I have another place in mind. It's that university and the twenties is usually the time you go out and get a taste of the world. That's how you find out what you like. Maverick Technologies, Shea Industries, Media Maven, and the record label are all global brands. We don't have to live in Evergreen for you guys to run your companies, and I can dance and be a therapist anywhere. I guess what I'm saying is, I love our lives the way it is now. But I'd still love it if it changed."

"Huh." Jaxson twisted me out and snapped me back, holding me secure under his arm. "I never thought about leaving. The truth is I'm happy anywhere there's a bed and you're naked and willing in it."

"Be serious," I said, laughing.

"I am. I'm good, Val. There's nowhere else I need to be."

Rising up, I pecked his jaw. "I'm happy to hear you say that. I feel the same."

The next morning, I woke early and climbed in the shower. Jaxson would no doubt be woken by the water and come in and join me, until then I took the time to think.

I was about to question Robert and Jolene Connelly. Aiden would hear about it. Maybe as soon as they closed the door behind me. What would he do?

Threaten me like he did Ezra? Threaten Maverick?

He's had years to do the first and weeks to do the second. He hasn't said a word.

Maybe that's what bothered me. The radio silence.

I didn't know where he, Sawyer, or Maverick were. I didn't know what they were doing. I didn't know if they were working to tear down Maverick's walls to reach that calm center. I didn't know because Aiden didn't have the decency to make a ransom call, gloat, hang around smirking. Something!

That is what I needed. Some confirmation he had Maverick and all I had to do was get through him. This silence I couldn't stand. Because all I could do was fill it with the worst thoughts.

"Val."

The curtain parted and Jaxson slipped in behind me. I leaned back in his arms.

"I looked up the address," he said. "They live close to the restaurant. We can walk."

"We'll go after breakfast. I won't wait longer than we have to."

My shower was meant to be relaxing. I stepped out tenser than ever, clenching and unclenching my fists. We dressed and went down for a breakfast buffet on the terrace. The whole time I flicked between the address on the screen and going over what I was going to say. My fiftieth check of the time was interrupted by the screen flashing a call.

"Hey, Ezra. Everything okay?"

"You always ask if everything is okay. Never how are you? Or what's up?"

"Blame it on our track record."

He chuckled. "Everything is okay. Big Moon and I are looking up acts to do his party."

"Big Moon?"

"Adam's new nickname."

My brows shot up my forehead. "Is that right? Big Moon sounds like the nickname for a frat boy who flashes his ass at everyone."

"He is turning seven," Ezra said like he was repeating it from a certain boy named Big Moon. "Can't call him baby anymore."

"We'll discuss new nicknames later. What's going on with the party?"

"You have to choose what kind of animals you want there. They don't show up with them all. I was thinking a petting zoo party. Adam is thinking lemurs."

I laughed. "How does he know what a lemur is?"

"We send him to a very advanced school."

"Let's do the petting zoo party and bribe the guy to bring a lemur or two for extra. Does that work for the big man?"

"I'll check." There was murmuring on the other end. "He accepts your terms."

"Put him on, please."

Adam came on the phone. I gushed all over him and said he'll always be my baby. By the time we ended the call, Jaxson was finished with his coffee and it was time to go.

He held out a hand for me. I took it and together we left.

The restaurant was no less busy during the breakfast rush. Servers and staff flitted about the place. Through the windows we didn't notice anyone who could be Aiden's middle-aged parents. We continued on to his house.

"It's number nineteen." I pointed to the home bearing a pink door and flower boxes along the porch banister. "Such a nice, normal place. What happened in that house to make Aiden... Aiden?"

"Maybe it's not what happened in that house, but what happened in the frat."

"Whatever he is mixed up in, he must believe it's worth the twenty-five to life he's got coming his way."

We climbed the steps to the porch. Jaxson stopped and nodded for me to go on.

Squaring my shoulders, I pressed the doorbell. I heard it chime through the house. Footsteps followed.

The door swung open, revealing Aiden Connelly in thirty years. I blinked at him. The resemblance was uncanny. There could be no doubt I was in the right place. This man was Aiden's father.

His eyes crinkled around the corners in curiosity—similar to Aiden's. "Hello? Can I help you?"

"Hi," I said, finding my voice. "My name is Valentina Moon, and this is my boyfriend, Jaxson. I don't know if Aiden ever mentioned me but I'm the president of Zeta Rho Sigma. We work closely together."

His eyes lit up. "Of course we've heard of you. Aiden's mentioned the woman who took Leighton's place was a firecracker. Nice to put the face to the stories."

I tensed. I don't know why his comment bothered me. It was good for me that his parents didn't see me as a total stranger crashing in on their life. But it didn't sit well that Aiden sat around chatting about me.

"Really? A firecracker?" I forced a laugh. "Don't know about that. I'm harmless."

"What brings you by?"

I dropped the smile. "I'm afraid it's serious. My boyfriend has gone missing and I was hoping I could ask you a couple questions."

"Boyfriend?" He flicked over my shoulder to Jaxson.

"My other boyfriend, Maverick Beaumont. Please, Mr. Connelly. I wouldn't be here if it wasn't important. Life or death."

"Life or death? I— Well— Yes," he said, stepping aside. "Of course you can come in.

"Jolene? Jolene," he called.

Jaxson and I went inside the rustic, mid-century modern home. The first thing that hit me as I passed through the front was Aiden, Aiden, and Aiden. Pictures of him from newborn to college graduation spanned the wall. Rounding the corner, I was freed of him to walk into the living room. Mr. Connelly gestured for us to sit while he went off in search of his wife.

Jaxson put his arm around me, kissing my crown. He didn't say more, and he didn't have to. He was here by my side. Everything would be okay.

"—matter of life or death."

"What?" The cry preceded a tall, short-haired woman entering the room. She rushed to my side. "Is everything okay? What's going on?"

"Hello, Mrs. Connelly. I'm sorry to just show up at your house like this, but I didn't know what else to do."

"Robert said your boyfriend is missing."

"Maverick Beaumont. He disappeared a few weeks ago after last being seen with a Nu Alpha guy, Sawyer Burn. I know the police asked you about—"

Her brows crumpled. "Police? We haven't spoken to the police."

"You haven't?" Jaxson and I swung to each other, sharing wide-eyed looks. "Officer Mylow said he contacted you and the dean to confirm Aiden was out sick."

She and Robert shook their heads. "We haven't heard from an Officer Mylow. Aiden did call us to say he was under the weather and taking time off, though."

"He did," I said slowly. I resisted another look at Jaxson. "Did you speak to him or did he leave a message?"

"A message. Why? What is this about?"

"It's why I'm here. Maverick, Sawyer, and Aiden all disappeared the same night. Maverick's parents also received a message that he was stressed and needed time off, but Maverick would never run off and leave me and our son. I'm very sorry to tell you this," I said as they lowered themselves in the armchairs. "I wished Officer Mylow spoke to you like he claimed he did. But I believe there's more to their being gone. They were kidnapped."

"What?"

"That's absurd!"

They both shouted at once.

I told Jaxson I'd both lie and tell the truth. The truth about Maverick, and lies about Aiden. His parents were unlikely to help me if I came in accusing their son of being a kidnapping psychopath. I'd be shown the door faster than I could blink.

"I know this is hard to hear," I continued. "I'm a stranger walking in here and throwing you into a parent's worst nightmare. Trust that I wouldn't have flown all the way here if I wasn't certain. I'm even more certain now that I've found out Mylow is a liar."

Jolene put her hands up. "Slow down. What are you saying? Someone's taken Aiden and... the police are covering it up? What about the message he left? I know my son's voice."

"I know Maverick's voice. Supposedly he had time to leave a voicemail on his parents' phone, but none to call and let me know he's okay? It doesn't make any sense."

"That doesn't mean he's been kidnapped," Robert said.

"It wouldn't if you didn't know Maverick. Or that Leighton Lewis was involved with shady people before she died."

"Leighton?" Jolene tossed her head as if trying to deflect all the things coming at once. "What shady people?"

"It's hard to explain. Now that she's gone, there's no one to prove what happened. All I know is she was involved in something illegal and had 'friends' covering her tracks. I found out before she died. Since I've taken over as president, I've tried to find out what she got the sorority mixed up in. Maverick offered to help me and he then vanished in a parking lot.

"This isn't random, Mrs. Connelly. It's not a coincidence that as we were getting closer, Maverick leaves the same way Leighton did. Nor do I think it's a coincidence Sawyer and Aiden took 'time off' that night too. The three of them must have been together in the parking lot when all of this happened."

Robert squeezed his wife's knee, penning in what she'd been about to say. "I see why you came to the conclusion that something may have happened to your boyfriend. Especially if you were taking matters into your own hands instead of leaving them to the police. You're afraid and feeling guilty, but there's nothing to suggest our son is involved. I'm certain the police did not contact us because they know there isn't a sign of foul play, and they didn't see a need to frighten us."

"Has this happened before?" I asked. Between our thighs, I linked pinkies with Jaxson. "Aiden's gone out of reach and all he's left is a voicemail."

"Yes," he replied. "Aiden is a grown man. He doesn't have to tell us where and when he goes, but still he always gives us a heads-up that he'll be unavailable."

"He hasn't been on campus. Aiden's vice president has been running the house while he's out. If he's not in Nu Alpha and he isn't home, where could he be?" I asked. "I'd feel a lot better if I could talk to him. See for myself that he's okay."

"Oh, did you not know Aiden has an apartment off campus?" Jolene went into the kitchen. "He prefers peace and quiet to study, so he stays there during finals and big projects to get out of the noisy frat house." Jolene came back holding a slip of paper. "He'll be there. As for your boyfriend, I'm sure everything's okay."

I stared at the slip. After all this time and weeks of cursing Aiden Connelly, was I finally handed the key to revealing who this man was and, more importantly, who he was involved with? Aiden never said a word about an off-campus apartment.

What are you keeping in there, Aiden?

Or who?

"Thank you." I took the address tentatively like she might snatch it away. "Who knows? Maybe Aiden's heard from Sawyer too and there's a reasonable explanation for why he hasn't been around. I just want to find Maverick. Every day without him is crushing me."

"Oh, dear," she tutted, rubbing my arm. "I can see how scared you are. Are you certain Leighton was involved with illegal activity? Maybe you misread the situation."

"I'm sure. I confronted her and she didn't bother to hide it. She said she was doing what she had to do, and I couldn't understand because I wasn't president. I was trying to find out who she was working with and then... this happened."

Jolene hugged me, murmuring words of comfort. Compassion and empathy rolled off her. You wouldn't have guessed this was the woman who birthed the likes of Aiden "Smirking" Connelly.

"I wish we could do more to help. Robert?"

"Have you reported Leighton's crimes to the police?" Mr. Connelly asked.

"We've been trying to get them to listen to us for years. Their 'investigations' go nowhere and I'm left with no answers and no boyfriend."

"If what you're saying is true," he replied, "I'd go over this Mylow's head and report him to his superiors. Leighton Lewis confessed to a crime. That should be handled with the seriousness it demands. Have that man removed from the case and given to another officer. If needed, we'll back your complaint and tell them you were lied to about Mylow contacting us."

Jolene nodded. "It's unthinkable giving you false progress reports while you're worried sick about your boyfriend. No wonder you flew all the way out here to see—"

The door creaked open.

"Mom? Dad, you home?"

My eyes widened.

"I'm taking my finals online. Figured I could do them here just as easily as..." Our gazes locked.

For the first time since the oily bastard came into my life, true, genuine shock blew up those handsome features. He looked from me, to Jaxson, to his parents, and then back to me—mouth open and waiting to end his sentence.

"Aiden," his mom said, rising to her feet. "Perfect timing, sweetie. Valentina was just asking about—"

Aiden turned tail, and ran.

"Hey!" I took off in pursuit.

I didn't think. I didn't hear Jaxson or the Connellys shouting after me. There was only one thing on my mind.

Skidding into the hall, I saw Aiden jump over the bushes and spring across the neighbor's lawn.

"Aiden!"

I gave chase in his wake. Jumping over the bushes. Running past the lawn gnomes. Picking up speed when he looked back to see me on his heels and ran faster.

"Why are you running, Connelly? Where's Maverick?!"

The Connellys' tucked-away neighborhood bordered the main street that led to their restaurant and the rest of town. I expected him to run into the hustle of people.

Aiden veered and ran through the street.

Honks broke the peaceful morning. A car swerved to avoid him and rear-ended someone in the other lane. Aiden raced for the tree line.

He's trying to lose me in the woods. Or worse, if he jumps in water, I won't be able to follow.

"Val, don't!"

I leaped off the sidewalk into the street.

A car zoomed past me, so close the mirror swiped across my stomach. Screaming, my heart smashed into my rib cage.

"Val!" Jaxson roared.

A brief stop was all Aiden needed to pull ahead. He broke through the trees, looking back once more at me. I swore he smirked.

"I'll get him!"

Feet pounding. Horns blaring. Angry shouts in my ear. I swerved through traffic and made it to the bank. Aiden was yards ahead of me and making straight for the lake. It wasn't a far swim to the forest on the other side, but it might as well have been miles to me.

He can't get to that water. Maverick needs you. Go!

I ran faster than I ever had in my life. My arms sliced the air. Breaths ripped from my lungs, and I gained on him.

Aiden reached the water and I jumped. Soaring through the air, I tackled him, pitching us both headfirst into the lake.

"Ahh!" Our shouts turned to gurgles—the lake rushed into our mouths.

Aiden thrashed trying to buck me off him. I wrapped around his waist and neck in a strangling grip, holding on for my life and Maverick's.

We burst over the surface.

"Get off, you crazy bitch!"

I fisted his hair and yanked his head back. "Where is Maverick? I know you took him. Tell me where he is!"

"Argh!"

"Tell me!"

He buried his elbow in my gut. The blow rocked my body, trapping the gasp in my throat. My grip loosened and Aiden took his chance.

He peeled me off, lifted me overhead, and flung me deeper into the lake. I sunk beneath the depths.

Aiden's hit stunned me. My body's desperation to catch my breath clashed with the need to hold it. I dropped to the rocky bottom of the lake.

A hand entered my vision and grabbed me. Jaxson hauled me out of the water.

"Val? Val, are you okay? Breathe, baby."

I did. I sucked in lungfuls of air, chest heaving as I clung to him tighter than Aiden.

"We've got to stop doing this," he said, holding me just as secure.

My laugh was half sob. "Did you see where he went?"

"I wasn't fucking worried about him! Val, what were you thinking? You were almost flattened, then drowned. We can't rescue Maverick if we're dead."

Jaxson's scolding faded in the background.

There.

Over his shoulder, a flash of movement disturbed the peaceful forest. Aiden.

"Jaxson." I clamped his jaw and smashed a rough kiss on his lips. "I love you and you're absolutely right. But he rabbited out of there at the sight of us for a *reason*. He knows where Maverick is, and if we let him get away, we'll never forgive ourselves."

"I didn't see where he went."

"That way." I pointed. "You go around and try to cut him off. He may slow down now that he thinks he's shaken us off."

"What if he goes home? We should wait there for him."

"No, he'd expect that." I'd have broken away and been gone after him by now but there was still the matter of not being able to swim.

"Plus, I doubt the Connellys will serve us tea and cookies while we wait to ambush their son. I'm not waiting any longer, Jaxson. Please, we need to go now."

"Alright." He swam us back, holding me close. "Our cellphones are both fucked, so if you catch up to him before I do, shout, scream, tell me where you are. I'll come running."

"Okay."

"He's lived here his whole life. He knows this forest better than us." Jaxson carried me to the shore. "Don't run around blind. Find his trail and follow it."

"I will. I love you."

"Love you."

Soaked and chilled to the bone, I did what Jaxson said, looking for Aiden's footprints while he looped around to get ahead. Almost immediately I found the deep grooves in the damp earth.

"Gotcha, son of a bitch. I'm getting my damn boyfriend back."

I didn't run this time. I followed the clear trail, letting it lead me straight to the shit-shitting bastard. He'd have to stop running eventually. That's when I'd be there to beat the smirk permanently off his face.

A twig snapped in the distance. I looked around, saw no one, and continued on.

Aiden clearly wasn't expecting me to go this far. Literally, I flew upstate to knock on his parents' door and have them tell me they knew even less about their son than I did.

Good thing I did. Aiden wasn't planning to come back this semester. I would've waited almost two months for a confrontation we'd have today.

Where was Maverick? If Aiden was here bumming the guest room off his parents, did that mean he wasn't the one keeping an eye on the captive? Did he leave Maverick in someone else's hands, or was Maverick locked up in his secret apartment at 101 Cypress Lane? The paper may have been a soggy wad in my pocket, but I seared the address in my memory.

Paradise Hills. Apartment 203B.

I'd be there as soon as I had Aiden.

Something flashed out of the corner of my eye. I whipped around, scanning a uniform sea of brown and green. "Aiden?"

His footsteps led farther up ahead. There was a chance he doubled back.

"I'm not playing these games anymore." I tread closer. "You wouldn't have run, hit me, or thrown me in a fucking lake if you were as innocent as you've been pretending—"

Caw!

A black mass shot off the ground. I shrieked, stumbling back as the raven winged it out of there.

Catching my breath, I couldn't help a chuckle. I was talking to birds and chasing fraternity presidents through the forest. So much for a normal college experience.

I turned back to the trail. The branch swung toward my face.

Pain erupted in my skull. I went down, hitting the roots of the tree to knock the wind out of me again.

A blurry shape stood over me. I think they were speaking though the roaring in my ears did not let the words through.

Aiden?

Darkness crept in around the edges, swallowing them as they grew bigger, kneeling over me.

No, my mind whispered.

Leighton.

Chapter Four

R*yder*

"What? How did you let that happen? Where the fuck were you, Jaxson?"

"Don't start," Jaxson snapped. "I've been cursing myself for letting her go after him alone all day. What matters is our gig playing detective is *over*." I got the sense that wasn't said just for my benefit. "Jacob and his guys are handling it from here. When they catch up to him, they'll fuck his face up even worse."

"He hit her in the face?" I shouted.

"Jaxson," Val cried through the speakers. "My face is not fucked up." There was noise and then Val came on the phone. "I have a bump on my forehead. The doctor checked me out and said I don't have a concussion. Everyone can relax."

"He. Is. Dead," I hissed.

"It might... not have been Aiden."

"What?"

"I think I saw— Whoever did it knelt down to speak to me. It was for half a second, but I swore I saw Leighton."

"Leighton? Leighton Lewis?" I repeated. "The woman who murdered a man in front of you—I've got a medal I need to give her for that—and then may or may not have faked her death? Why would she be running through the forest of St. Germaine?"

"I don't have a clue," Valentina confessed. "My vision was going. It might have been Aiden and my mind played tricks on me. I know it's crazy that she would be there. Doesn't make sense."

"Are you trying to convince yourself or me?"

"Both."

I left the kitchen. I was in the middle of making pizza bites for Adam. Chef offered to do it, but Adam insisted I "made it better." Flattering. Untrue, but still flattering, and by now the kid knew flattery is what it took to get me in an apron.

The kid in question lay under his blanket fort with Pepper zonked out in front of him and Cara curled up on his back. I returned to the kitchen, safe that he couldn't hear me.

"Okay, let's say it was her," I began. "What does that mean? Has Lewis been there all this time? Or did she follow you?"

"Neither makes any sense. I don't know a lot about her, but I know she isn't from St. Germaine. Her only connection to this place is Aiden, but why would Aiden have her stashed away here instead of his secret apartment?"

I would follow up on the secret apartment later. "So, she followed you."

"How could she do that? She didn't know we'd be here. It's not like the woman hid behind a baggage cart at the airport. We flew your mom's jet."

"You're right," I muttered. "She couldn't have known you'd be there. But all three of you in the same place, in the same forest..." I shook my head. "That's not a coincidence."

"I agree. I don't know what to believe, Ryder. I'm starting to think I did hallucinate her."

"The alternative is you're being stalked by a homicidal former sorority president who put a tracking chip in your neck, and knocked you out when you tried to take her boyfriend."

"Very helpful," Val deadpanned. "But if I didn't hallucinate, then that's exactly what happened. Why would Leighton try to stop me from getting to Aiden? How'd she know he needed saving?"

"Jacob is going to answer those questions. Jaxson's right. You're done." I picked up the bag of shredded cheese. "Do you know how bad this could've been if Jaxson wasn't there? The fucker tossed you in a lake. He left you unconscious on the ground. It was one thing when he was content to drop veiled hints. Now he's gotten physical. We're handling this from here on."

"We? I thought Jacob was handling it."

"Jacob will find him. Jaxson, Ezra, and I will take over from there. By the time we're done with him, we'll know where Maverick is."

"I won't be sidelined. I told you I'm not sitting on my ass anymore, and I meant it." Valentina heaved a sigh. "It's been a long day and we still have to pack and fly out. I'm pretty sure Aiden's going to avoid his parents' house in case any more surprises are waiting for him. If we're unlucky, and so far we have been, they'll tell him that we know about the apartment.

"Jaxson wouldn't let me do anything but see a doctor and lie in this bed. If Aiden took off after our run-in with him, he'll be close to home by now. You're there, Ryder. You need to see inside his apartment before him."

"You mean break in."

"I do," she said clearly.

"Good. Give me the address."

I STOPPED IN FRONT of the sign for Paradise Hills Luxury Apartments.

Finishing up the pizza bites and handing the rest over to Chef took minutes. Kissing Mom goodbye and asking her to look after Adam took less than that. Telling Ezra Val needed us and to get his ass in the car took seconds.

"How do we know he lives alone?" Ezra remarked. "The guy could have a secret girlfriend or boyfriend to go with the secret apartment."

"We don't know. We do know it takes five hours to drive here from St. Germaine. It's been longer than that since he attacked Val. We may already be too late."

"Let's not waste any more time. Know how to get in?"

I nodded.

Luxury apartments tended to have key fob entry. Paradise was no different. A white sedan drove up and let themselves in through the gate. We rode their bumper inside, then drove around looking for his apartment.

"Chances Maverick's locked in the guest room?" Ezra spoke up. "What are we looking for in there?"

"It's not a question by now that shit's mixed up in something and now Maverick and Val are in on it too. We haven't got a thing on this guy." I parked in an empty space. "Even his parents are repeating the official story."

"Think they were lying?"

"I think everyone's lying," I replied as we climbed out. "Question is why. What's everybody working so hard to cover up? Did Val tell you Mylow's been giving us false reports?"

Ezra bobbed his head. "What can you do? Some people are desperate to get fired."

"We'll help him out."

The complex was clean, quiet, and well-maintained. Not a student apartment and not cheap by the looks of it.

"How does Connelly make his money?" Ezra voiced my thought out loud.

"Don't know. Jacob's trying to get information on him, but he's locked his stuff down as tight as Maverick. I don't have anyone with his hacking skills on the payroll. Val says the family restaurant is successful. Maybe Mom and Dad are paying his way."

"If he is on someone's payroll, it would explain some things. Not much, but it'd make sense that he's not doing this alone. I mean, he can't be. It's been going on since he was a kid."

"That's the worst part of this. We can't identify the other players. Is it the alumni or chapter members? Is it an outside group? Is it a fucking group? Connelly gave a story about researching athletes and getting them to their peak performance. Men, women, different builds, different sports, different backgrounds. They may all be test groups."

203B loomed ahead of us.

"You ever notice," Ezra asked, "that it never works out well for the guinea pigs?"

I didn't answer. Because I have noticed.

"There's a camera," I said, avoiding a direct look. "Stand in the way. Keep talking to me and mess with your phone."

"Can you break in?"

I examined the lock. "Standard Yale. Shouldn't be a problem."

Ezra turned his back, shielding me as I bent over the metal with my picks.

"Since when do you know how to do this?"

"Jacob taught me. It's part of his contract to run drills with me and Mom in case we're ever in a kidnapping situation. Getting out of the ropes doesn't matter if you can't get out of the room."

"Smart. We need to do that with Val and Adam."

"Way ahead of you. Our first drill is in January— Got it." Carefully, I turned the lock to the sweet sound of the bolt sliding free.

"Wait."

I halted with my hand on the knob.

"This guy's been careful so far. He could have an alarm system or more cameras inside to prove we've gone from harassing him to breaking and entering."

"I have faith in my thousand-dollar-an-hour lawyers." I threw the door open. "Don't you?"

Ezra mumbled something under his breath. I went in and then him after me, closing the door behind.

We stood in a darkened hallway. My vision slowly adjusted.

A low whistle cut through the silence.

"Damn," said Ezra. "Whoever's paying this guy, they've got more money than us. Combined."

An exaggeration, but not that big of one. Aiden Connelly outfitted himself with all the finishes.

His television covered an entire living room wall—retailing at sixteen thousand dollars. I knew this because I was getting one for our bedroom as a Christmas present for Val. Anything to keep her in our bed longer.

Aiden didn't stop at the television. The entertainment system to go with it was equally as impressive. Every gaming system on the market, and another wall dedicated to the shelves housing his games.

"Aiden didn't lie to his parents about this," I said. "This is where he goes to get away from watchful eyes and do what he wants. He's safe in this apartment, Ezra. If he's going to hide something, he'd do it here."

"The usual places?"

"I'll take the kitchen. You take the bathroom."

We split to start our search. There were an infinite number of places to hide something in an apartment. Like we'd come to accept, Aiden Connelly was clever. In all Jacob's digging, he didn't find this place.

But his parents knew about it. If there was ever a surprise visit from Mommy, he wouldn't have the whips and chains on display. He'd hide it, and be clever about it.

I checked the oven, boxes in the pantry, under the kitchen sink, and the freezer. I hit gold inside an old ice cream container.

"Ezra," I called.

"What do you got?"

I tipped the bag onto the counter. "Money. About ten grand cash."

"To go with the five grand I found taped under the sink," he said from the doorway, holding up the bills. "Not that scandalous considering we can see he has money."

"True, but regular, everyday law-abiding citizens tend to keep their money in a bank instead of a tub of mint chocolate chip."

"Thinking this guy is selling drugs? Pills? Performance enhancers?"

"Maybe. Not drugs, but if he's handing out steroids someone cooked up in their lab, it'd explain why he's keeping detailed notes on his brothers. They're a research project."

"Then, why do they go missing? Why did Maverick?" Ezra grew faint as he returned the money to its hiding place. "He'd never take a random pill from the guy he went in to spy on."

"We're assuming Aiden gave him a choice. Valentina said those files were on every guy in Nu Alpha. How often does Val cook and share meals with the sorority?"

"A university doping scandal could ruin a few careers." He came out, looking around. "And Connelly's got all this to lose."

"I'll look in the bedroom. Sweep the whole living room."

"I've got it."

Aiden's bedroom was grander than the living room. His California king bed took center stage, draped in expensive black sheets. A television only slightly smaller than the one outside towered over me while I checked his drawers.

Nothing but clothes. The closet held the same.

I tried his desk next. Decades in the company of Maverick Beaumont gave me a healthy knowledge of computers. I was looking at an Imperium 380X and I'd bet the mansion on it. Maverick's words came back to me.

"The 380X is the ultimate in cybersecurity. You can't turn it on without a fingerprint, password, and a key about the size of an SD reader. Even if you got through all of that, it's set up so you can protect certain files under advanced encryption.

"Photos of the family picnic sit free on the desktop, but company files can be flagged as important and locked away. Dad worked on part of the encryption and let me kick in some code. Only part of it though. They contracted several companies so no one would know how to beat it, and come up with a computer that could top it." He grinned. *"Doesn't mean we won't try."*

I backed away from the computer, not bothering to touch it. "Once again, we underestimate you, Connelly. You do keep your secrets in this apartment, and no one is getting to them but you."

Even so, not everything could be stashed in an encrypted folder. Not cold, hard cash, or—

My fingers brushed something smooth taped under the bed. I craned my neck to see the sheathed knife secured where it'd be in easy reach. A picture was beginning to form of this guy, and it wasn't reassuring. Guilt pressed in heavier than this bed collapsing on top of me.

We let Maverick walk into a situation we didn't understand, with people we didn't know a thing about. I should've insisted he had security follow him. I should've pushed for him to install the MT trackers he bragged about in his watch or shoe. This could've been prevented if we didn't always act first and think later when Val was concerned. All to protect her, we told ourselves, and now Maverick was missing and Val hurt worse than ever lying banged up in a hotel bed giving everything to find him.

"This is my fault," I hissed.

"Ryder!"

I jerked, banging my head on the frame. "Fuck, Ezra. What's your prob—?"

"He's here, Ryder. He's turning the key in the lock."

I scrambled under the bed, nearly knocking foreheads with Ezra as he dove in the other side.

"Did you close the—?"

He nodded roughly, holding a finger over his lips. He closed the bedroom door and hopefully the bathroom too. I could guess what a man hiding a knife and fifteen grand would do to trespassers. My thousand-dollar-an-hour lawyers couldn't get me off a blade through the chest.

"... was there... just got back..."

Footfalls thudded in the apartment. The television flicked on, playing what sounded like the news. I strained to hear over it. Was someone with Connelly or was he on the phone?

"—didn't have a choice!"

That I heard loud and clear.

"Don't give me that. It's your fucking fault."

Bang!

Aiden stormed in the room. I followed his feet under the slit in the bed curtain.

"She was at my parents' house. Sitting on the couch sipping tea and eating cookies like it was just another Saturday."

Ezra grabbed my shoulder. He needn't have. I knew exactly who he was talking about, and was listening hard.

"You were hired to keep her in check, Ortega. Today shouldn't have happened."

Our gazes locked through the dark, a single name going through our minds.

Jade.

"No. I said *no*," he barked. "She didn't find out anything from my parents because my folks don't know anything to tell. Moon is getting desperate. She chased me through town demanding I tell her where Beaumont is."

Where is Beaumont, you fuck? Say it!

"I lost her in the woods, made up some explanation for my parents, and drove straight back. We need to meet and discuss how we're going to handle the situation once and for all. This is the last time Moon fucks around in my life."

There was a pause while Jade spoke on the other end. The mattress dipped.

Thud. Thud.

Aiden kicked off his shoes. The rest of his clothes hit the floor.

"Don't start. I had to take Beaumont. He was perfect. He should've pledged Nu Alpha from day one. Snagging him was worth Moon's wrath at the time. Now it's getting old."

My lips peeled back from my teeth. This guy spoke of kidnapping Maverick and tearing a hole through our lives like reading from a grocery list. *I had to get milk, eggs, and cheese. We were out.*

None of this stirred his conscience in the slightest.

"You said you could handle her. So far, she's running around free and turning the Zetas... on... you. Hold on," he said. "Just hold on a second. I think... someone's been in here."

Every molecule in us froze.

"No, it's my drawer. It's cracked open."

I cursed myself six ways to Sunday. Stupid. Stupid, stupid, stupid!

"No one knows about this place except you, Martin, and my parents." He said the final word with a finality I didn't like. "I'll call you back."

It wasn't a surprise when the next number he called was home.

"You gave her my address? Why did you do that?" he gritted. "That's not the point. I told you to keep it to yourself. I'm not— I'm not yelling at you, Mom."

Pause.

"Okay, I'm sorry. It's not your fault. It's fine. I'll take care of it."

His bare feet moved across the carpet, going to the door. Aiden closed and locked it.

"If anyone's in here, show yourself," he said. "Don't make me find you."

I drifted to the knife. Inching back, I closed over the hilt.

"Valentina?" He ducked into the closet. "Didn't get enough? Came running back here for more?"

I drew the weapon from its sheath, riding a tide of swelling rage. This piece of shit wasn't fit to say her name. He wasn't fit to look at her.

Ezra's grip clenched on my shoulder.

I could end this right here. A jab to the ankle would drop him. Ezra and I would be on him while he's still screaming. Tie him with those silk sheets and carve him up until he's appropriately sorry for touching our girlfriend, and makes it up by revealing where Maverick is.

I glanced at Ezra. He pointed toward the desk and then jerked his head the other way. I understood better than if he said it out loud.

Wait till Connelly moves away from the door, then block his escape.

I slid the knife free.

"Jade."

We stilled.

"My mother gave up the address," he said, padding out of the closet. "I'm going to check the place and keep you on speaker. You hear anything, come over." Aiden dropped to his knees. "Moon's playing more games."

Damn this guy! I shoved the knife back in.

Tossing his head, Ezra gestured wildly and, past his shoulder, a hand grasped the hem of the bed skirt.

"Moon!" The skirt swished up. "Shit."

"What?" Ortega spoke up. "What's going on?"

"Nothing, it's cool. There's no one in the bedroom. I'll search the rest of the apartment."

Ezra and I didn't breathe in the corner between the wall and nightstand where we tucked ourselves. Aiden headed for the door. We crouched lower. All he had to do was turn around.

Aiden left without a backward glance.

"We could still try to get the phone off him," Ezra said. "You go for his hand, I go for his throat."

"Too risky. One shout and a witness is on her way. And we can't carry him out because of the cameras." We crept back under the bed. "We wait."

We did wait. For Aiden to search his place top to bottom, then come back telling Jade he was paranoid.

"Running into that bitch at my house set me on edge. I'm seeing short-haired, pouty nuisances in the shadows." From the drawers slamming, it sounded like he was finishing getting ready. "Tomorrow. What time are we meeting up?

"We have to put her down. She's becoming a problem. If you won't do it, I will," he snapped.

It was everything in me to not grab the knife and slice him up anyway.

Think first, react later. Val doesn't need one boyfriend missing and two in prison.

"Alright. Noon. Bye."

Another drawer slammed. Aiden left the room. After a few minutes, the shower turned on.

"Should we get him when he comes out?"

"No," I replied. "Ortega's expecting him tomorrow. If he shows up beat to shit, or doesn't show up at all, it'll be Valentina's name in her ear as the person he said was lurking in his apartment."

I stole out from under the bed and checked to make sure the living room was clear. We didn't speak till we were safely outside and making for the car.

"We need to be smart from here on," I said. "Smarter than Connelly because for fuck sure he's been ahead of us. Today was the first Valentina caught him off guard and it rattled him. Now that we know about this place, we'll get Jacob in while he's out to plant bugs. The next time he rants to Ortega about Valentina or Maverick, we'll hear it. When he pulls up whatever he's got on that computer, we'll see it."

"He's going to rant about Valentina tomorrow." Ezra cut me off and went for the driver's seat. "They're planning something to stop her for good! That's the conversation we need to hear."

"They're not going to hurt Val. At the sorority house, she's surrounded by sisters. At home, she's surrounded by us. They can't get her alone to touch her," I said. "My bet is they'll resort to threats."

"And they have the most effective one tucked away somewhere," Ezra said, following my line of thought. "Maverick."

"As long as they stick to empty threats, we'll have time to get the info we need to find him."

"We're only guessing those threats are empty, Shea. We don't know what the hell these people are doing to Maverick."

"You heard Connelly on the phone." We drove away from Paradise Hills and 203B.

"Pissed that Maverick didn't pledge the fraternity," I continued. "He said that Maverick was perfect, proving they're taking these people for a reason, and it was worth the heat coming down on them to grab him."

"You know, we've been thinking about this through the lens of bullshit Sawyer fed Maverick before he was taken. There are other reasons you go after attractive, well-built people. We could be dealing with human trafficking, Ryder. Maybe Maverick was perfect... because he was chosen."

I was silent. For too long.

"Ezra, whatever you do, do not tell Val that theory."

"Are we pretending she hasn't considered every possible worst-case situation?"

"We don't have to confirm it," I snapped.

"Then, just between you and me. The money. The knife. The security. What if we're dealing with something far more deadly, and it's been going on for years?"

"Maverick bought and sold?" The sentence burned my tongue. "I can't believe that. He's not the type a predator would usually go after. For ransom, yes. To be kept in the basement, no. He's smart, wealthy, connected, and strong enough to overpower them if they make a wrong move. These guys usually go for poor, isolated people who won't be looked for."

"Who's looking for Maverick, Ryder? Besides us. We can't even get the police to give a shit."

"But we are looking for him and we *will* find him. Val's forced them to reveal their hand before. We'll make them do it again."

VALENTINA

I sat in the dark, trailing my finger around the rim.

The flight back to Evergreen only lasted seventy-five minutes according to my watch. It felt ten times longer.

I went to St. Germaine to get answers, and walked away with more questions and a lump on my head. Despite Ezra's and Ryder's assurances when I got back and heard what happened in Aiden's place, I didn't feel any closer to finding Maverick.

"Valentina."

The porch flooded with light. Ezra came out holding a mug of his own.

"Saw the hot water on the stove and the door open. Put two and two together. Mind if I join you?"

"Of course not."

He set his cocoa next to mine and lifted my legs off the chaise. I smiled as he placed them on his lap, gently kneading my feet.

"Are you sure you're okay?"

"This?" I asked, pointing to my bandage. "This is nothing. I'm more freaked out about the person I think gave it to me."

Ezra blew out a breath. "This whole situation is so bizarre. I keep waiting for the camera crew to pop out and say *surprise, we're filming a horror movie and you're the stars.*"

"Our lives do seem to lurch from one disaster to another." He squeezed in, enfolding me in his arms. I rested my head on his shoulder. A bit of my tension leaked away.

"Remember that game we played on the roof that night?"

"Yes," I whispered. "I discovered all the secrets of Ezra Lennox."

"All of them? You sure?"

"All of these years and a son later, I better have."

He laughed. "Try me."

I saw this for the distraction it was and dove in eagerly. For a minute I didn't want to think about how I was no closer to finding Maverick, but seemingly in more danger than ever.

"Okay, you're on." I sipped my cooling cocoa, searching my mind for the scant topics I didn't know about Ezra. It was hard to believe there was a time I found him as dark and enigmatic as his eyes. Now I knew everything from his favorite shaving cream to his wearing socks to sleep because his feet are always cold.

"Your mom's company," I began. "Was it your dream to become the next Media Maven? Or did you hope to build something of your own?"

Of course, we talked about his dreams and plans for the future. He talked so animatedly about it, I didn't question that he wanted it, and I was sure he did, but it was possible deep down...

"I've thought about it." Ezra kissed the sensitive spot under my ear. "Most people don't have to think about these things, but the problem I faced was the same one Maverick, Jaxson, and Ryder had. Our parents' businesses. Their lives. It's all we know. It's what we've been raised to do.

"If we strike out on our own, we're looking at being in competition with our parents. Even worse, the companies have to go to someone.

If I'm not the next Media Mogul, someone else takes my birthright. If journalism wasn't all I've wanted to do, I wouldn't care, but this is what I'm meant for."

I hummed. "I guess that's true. Most people don't have to think about their parents as either partners or rivals."

"My turn," he said. "Do you think it's time you learned how to swim?"

"Ezra," I cried, smacking his thigh. "You can't shake that dark sense of humor."

His chuckles faded. "I say it like it's a joke, but I mean it, Val. Let us teach you. Please. I don't want to think what would've happened if Jaxson wasn't there."

I sighed. "I don't want to think what would've happened either. Yes, it is time I learned how to swim." I wiggled on him. "Will you reward my progress with pool sex?"

"That's a given."

"Then, we can start whenever you're ready."

Ezra interrupted my laugh with a kiss. Light and sweet, he nibbled on my bottom lip and scraped it between his teeth. My moan ratcheted up with the heat pooling between my legs.

"My turn," I said against his lips. "This. The way the five of us are right now. Do you think we'll last?"

His smile dimmed. "Wow. We are digging deep with these questions. Where did that come from?"

"It's your turn to answer." My voice was soft.

He carded his fingers through his hair. "Dammit, okay. I think... I think there'll be hard days. We'll have a houseful of kids and clash on how to raise them. Choosing a family vacation will require meetings, voting, and a mediator. Every day I'll want more of you, and some days I'll resent that your attention is divided elsewhere. We'll fight, slam doors, and argue about petty things. Then, we'll make up, remember our family is the one we've always wanted, and I'll know every second I get to spend with you is enough for a lifetime."

Ezra caught my heart as it was sinking. He kissed a tear running down my cheek, smearing my lips salty.

"We'll last, Val. The five of us are destined to be on this porch in seventy years—hips all broken from the dirty stuff we keep doing to your fine, wrinkled ass."

A snort burst out of me, riding a wave of giggles. Just the vision of us ninety years old and still getting it on in the back seat was enough to do it.

"I don't doubt it for a minute, Val. We'll last."

"Good." I smiled. "I don't doubt it either."

"My turn," he said, rubbing his nose on mine. "How hot do you think we'll be at ninety? Ryder's losing that head of hair for sure. Bald as an egg."

"No way. Silver fox."

"These eyes you love so much," he said, pointing to himself. "They'll become milky, rheumy things. Jaxson will have a beer gut. Maverick will pop his teeth out at the dinner table."

I laughed so hard I teared up for another reason. "I take it back. We don't have to last that long."

"Too late. You're stuck with us."

"Are you sure? I can't trade in for younger models?"

"You can try. I guarantee you'll outlive them."

"Oooh." Twisting around, I straddled him, draping my arms over his shoulders. "Guess I am stuck with you guys. It's a good thing I'm ridiculously in love with you."

"Whose question is it? Because I've got one. Do you remember the other thing we did on the roof?"

I hummed. "Counted the stars?"

"Nope."

"Ate brownies?"

"That's not it." Ezra slipped under my dress, tugging my panties aside.

"Bared our souls to each other and fell in love."

"Bared is right."

Ezra slid two fingers inside of me, drawing a moan from my lips. "Oooh. Now I remember, you fingered me till I soaked those fancy dress pants and sullied the image of the always perfect and put-together Ezra."

"Sweetie, your cum could only improve my image, not sully it." He stretched me to the brim. "I'll take some more if you're offering."

"You've never had to wait for an offer," I teased.

"Damn right. Why start now?"

Ezra disappeared. He dropped down between my legs so fast, I squealed.

Gripping my ass, he brought me down to his mouth.

It was wild that after years together and many, many times with his head between my legs, I still quivered with excitement like I did that first night—just me and Ezra on the roof.

He split me with his tongue, plundering my folds to heat me up on the cool night. I rocked a little. Moving up and down, I impaled myself on him, nipples firming to rock-hard points beneath my thin fabric.

Ezra smacked my ass.

"Eep," I squeaked.

My muscles contracted around him, racing toward orgasm. Hot breath on my clit, hands tormenting my ass, tongue fucking me in all the right spots. It wasn't reasonable for me to hold out under these conditions. I came screaming on top of him.

Ezra winked. "You still taste so sweet."

"Thank you." I wiggled down and kissed him. "You still have me dropping my panties outside. We will be just as bad when we're ninety."

"I'm looking forward to it."

Ezra curled his arm behind his head and used the other to pull me between him and the chair. I settled on his chest, closing my eyes as I inhaled his distinctly Ezra scent. The cost of his imported cologne is more than Mom and I used to see in a month. Just the smell of him coming around the corner quickened my pulse. Money well spent.

I woke hours later to the sun cresting over the trees and Ezra wrapped around me. I lay there for a while, tracing his face and thinking.

Ezra and Ryder told me what they found, and heard, in Aiden's apartment. He and Jade were planning to *handle* me. Make sure I don't show up in any more living rooms or chase any other presidents out through the streets.

Did that mean I was next to be picked up? Was it wrong that part of me hoped that was their plan? If I was taken to Maverick, I'd get him out. I'd get us both out.

Wishful thinking.

It won't be that easy. It never is with Aiden, or with Jade. Both of which look at me with barely concealed anger simmering beneath the surface. They were discussing putting me down for good. Whether that meant violence, blackmail, or both, I had to be ready.

The truth of that passed through my head, stirred no emotion, and went out. Years of this, it all had to come to a climax eventually and I'd been actively trying to push it there. I'm not surprised Aiden is fed up. I wanted him to be. I wasn't surprised Jade was ready to get rid of me. I wanted her to try.

I was ready for their next move. If anything, I was cool with them hurrying up.

Chapter Five

I reclined on the window seat, sharing a plate of cookies with Sofia. Down below, the Nu Alphas jumped in and out of the pool, playing what looked like a land- and water-based game that involved water guns, tackling, and nearly knocking into Aiden at the grill three times.

The first day of the start of winter break Aiden threw a barbecue for the guys who decided to stay on campus rather than go home. Surprisingly, he was one of them.

"Maybe we should take the sisters and join them," Sofia said. "Aiden's face these days whenever you're in the same room is priceless."

"By priceless you mean constipated."

We snorted, almost choking on our cookies.

Two weeks since Aiden returned to the fraternity. Two weeks we were both focused on finals—though my attention was split on my family, Maverick, and Aiden's impending attack. While Aiden was thinking who knows what.

Two weeks I waited for him or Jade to make a move, and neither one so much as spoke to me outside of fraternity business. It was like St. Germaine never happened.

"What is he waiting for?" I whispered, staring at the hard ridges and coiffed head of hair that made up the back of him.

"This," said Sofia. "Most of the brothers and sisters are gone. The two weeks you've been surrounded by people. Now there are three women left in the house. One of them Jade."

I drew the curtains closed on him. "You make a very good point, Sofia Richards. Disturbing, but accurate. Now is the time to grab me if they were planning to do it while I'm in the Sally house."

"Remind me why we want that again?"

"We've stalled, Sofia. Jacob put men on Aiden the day after he came back. He also broke into his apartment and bugged the place. Aiden hasn't driven off and led them to where he's keeping Maverick. He hasn't spoken a suspicious word in his apartment to himself or anyone over the phone. Jade continues to look at me like I'm a nutcase whenever I demand she tell me the truth.

"Adam's birthday is in a week and I promised him his dad would be home by then. I will not break that promise." I picked up another cookie, crumbling it into a chocolate chip mess on the plate. "I had to force them into making a move. Every day we're in limbo, who knows what is happening to Maverick?"

"You did force them into doing something. They went out for tea, cookies, and a chat about how to put you down for good. Val, what if this gets very ugly, very fast?"

I smiled at her. "You can help me with that, best friend. Did you find Jade's sisters? What did they say?"

Her expression changed, broadcasting a smile of her own. "These last few weeks, I've been chatting with Luna, Elizabeth, and Nora. They were all in the same pledge class as Jade. Nora and Luna came to the fundraiser. I made up a story about us organizing another event and making it more of a reunion. The theme is where the sisters are now and what they were doing back in the day. They're all very excited."

"What did they say about Jade?"

"I haven't asked them directly," she admitted. "We don't know who's involved in this, and coming right out and asking for Jade's secret might end up with one of them calling and telling her what we're doing."

"What have you been talking about, then?"

Sofia flapped a hand. "Us. I've told them all about these last few years and some of the secrets that came out that night. No names. Just a lot of *how did they find out a father had a second family* and *how did they know a mom passed corporate secrets?*" she said. "Pretending like I was just making conversation. Luna and Nora didn't take the bait, but Elizabeth did."

I rose off my bottom leaning in to hear. "And?"

"Elizabeth was equally horrified by what her president dug up on the pledges. She said one sister ran crying from the room when she was forced to read that she was adopted. She did not know before that day." Sofia pulled a face. "Another sister was close to her brother. Very, *very* close."

"Incest?" I hissed.

Sofia nodded.

"Why in the hell would she read that out for everyone to hear? Getting into the Sallys couldn't have meant that much to her?"

"According to Elizabeth, they did things differently back in the day. The choices were read your card and get in, or we'll read it for you and kick you out."

My mouth fell open. "Wow. It's truly amazing to me that the Sally and Sam pledge classes didn't drop to zero years ago. Why put up with this stuff?"

Sofia rubbed my arm. "Hazing has been going on for a long time, Val. People still join frats and sororities. It's only now we're starting to see a difference. Back then, the sisters put up with it, then they turned around and participated."

"Okay," I said, blowing out a breath. "Adoption and incest. What else did we get?"

"An SAT cheating scandal that was covered up by their rich mommy and daddy. One sister that was secretly married and also cheating on said secret husband. Two sisters that hid high school pregnancies and gave their kids up for adoption. One with a history of sticky fingers whenever they walked into a department store. And the last one Elizabeth mentioned was a sister who bullied a classmate in high school. She and her friends were relentless making this poor girl miserable till eventually she committed suicide."

"Oh my goodness, that's awful."

"It is awful." Sofia rested on the frame. "Elizabeth was honest. She said they were all friends before that night. After, it was hard to look anyone in the eye. The next four years in the Sally house, they went through the motions of bonding activities and morning runs, but no one truly felt comfortable. She asked the same question I've been asking myself, Val.

"Why do they put us through that initiation? It's not to foster sisterhood or trust no matter what bullshit they spew. I can't help but think—"

"It's to keep us afraid," I finished. "Always in the back of our minds scared of what they could do to us if we complain, tell people something is wrong, betray the secrets we stumble over. I've thought the same thing too."

We were quiet for a beat.

"Well, that's what she's told me so far," Sofia spoke up. "I didn't want to push it and make her wary, but we know some brutal secrets about her sisters, and one of them could be Jade."

"The trick is finding out which one. Was she the thief or the cheater? Did she give up a baby or cheat on her husband? Is she sleeping with her brother? If she was the one who was adopted, we have nothing. It's hardly blackmail material, especially now that the truth is out."

I balled my fists. "They use our secrets to keep us afraid. I'll use hers to kill any plans of silencing me, and skipping straight to her telling me where Maverick is."

"I can come right out and ask," said Sofia. "She might tell me."

I shook my head. "She has no reason to tell you. Plus, like you said, it may get back to Jade. We'll have to figure it out ourselves."

"Might not be too hard. Jacob is digging into her life. Does she have siblings? Are her parents wealthy? We can check two right off with those answers."

I was already fishing out my phone. Jacob answered on the third ring.

"Miss Moon. Is everything all right?"

"Everything is fine. I'm calling because I have a few questions about Jade. Do you have a minute to talk?"

"I do. What do you want to know?"

I went through asking all the questions about Jade's background I could think of. By the end of the conversation, we narrowed the list as much as we could.

"She doesn't have a brother, so that's out," I read off Sofia's list. "Mr. and Mrs. Ortega veer upper-middle class. They must have a nice chunk of spare change lying around, but I wouldn't classify them as rich, or think they'd have enough for a bribe that a teacher or principal would risk their job."

"Depends on how desperate that teacher or principal was," Sofia said. She squished in next to me to read over my shoulder. "If they were in debt and about to be kicked out of their apartment, a couple thousand could be a rent payment."

"True," I mumbled. I wrote *cheater* under Jade's name. "She could be one of the women who got pregnant in high school."

"I heard doctors can tell if a woman's given birth before, but we for fuck sure can't. How would we find out?" Sofia rested her head on my shoulder. "You know better than anyone that you can hide a pregnancy from everyone around you if you're really determined."

"It would be hard to prove. Asking Jacob to dig up adoption records covering all four years in her hometown is asking for him to spend the next six months buried in files." I sighed. "Plus, I wouldn't stretch this to blackmail. It's not like choosing a loving family to take care of your child is something to be ashamed of. And I wouldn't track down the child and throw them into this mess. They don't deserve that." I scratched out secret pregnancies. "I'm crossing my fingers Jade isn't one of those two sisters. I need leverage I can use."

"All we have left is the thief, the bully, and the secret husband." Sofia took the notepad and pen. "Jacob said she went to North Peak High School. There's nothing online about a student committing suicide, but he'll keep looking."

"She could be the shoplifter," I offered. "But it comes back to if that's enough to force her to tell us the truth."

"I wouldn't give up my secrets for a handful of petty crimes that's in my past."

"If it is in the past. Think she still has tags on those oversized candles and yoga mats?"

We cracked up. "What's really messed up is one girl was forced to reveal an incestuous relationship while the other says she pocketed a few lipsticks from Sephora. Not equal at all."

I had to agree. "What can you do? Some people live more colorful lives than others do. I mean, your big secret wasn't even yours."

"Hey," Sofia cried. "Are you saying my life isn't colorful?"

"Are you kidding? I'm saying their network of spies don't know everything. The crap we dealt with in Evergreen... Our lives are all the colors of the rainbow."

"Scarily true." She settled back down. "So, the cheater or the bully. Those secrets may not be enough to wreck her life, but I bet they'd get her kicked out of Somerset. How would the dean justify keeping a woman who cheated on the SATs to get into this school, or drove a student to kill themselves?"

"Can't be justified. Jade would be out, and I have a feeling the people who put her here wouldn't be too pleased. The hard part now is proving one of those secrets is hers. If not, we're back where we started."

"Where we started is still better than where we were."

I parted the curtains, looking down at Aiden. "Is it?" I muttered. "From where I'm sitting, Aiden is still a free man holding all the cards, and Maverick is who knows where being put through who knows what."

"Let's snatch a few of those cards, babe." Sofia dropped her feet on the floor. "Come with me and follow my lead."

Confused, I trailed her out the door. Sofia led me down to the kitchen, threw open the fridge, and pulled out ingredients. "I think we've got everything for you to make your famous Italian sausage tortellini soup."

"What?"

"Lindsay! Ivy!" she called. "We're making lunch. Want some?"

"What's on the menu?" one of them shouted back.

"Sausage tortellini."

Rapid footsteps thundered down the stairs. Lindsay and Ivy breezed in.

"You spoil us, Prez," Ivy said. "What do you want us to do?"

I looked to Sofia for some kind of clue. She threw big eyes back at me.

"Chop the onions and garlic," I finally said. "I'll do the sausage."

We got to work, grabbing knives, cutting boards, and aprons.

"What are you guys doing over break?" Sofia asked.

"Not much," Lindsay replied. "I've got a huge research project due at the start of the semester. There are five kids in the house, so it's not a great place to study, let alone try to hold a thought in your head for more than a second. I'm staying here to finish it, and on Christmas, I'll drive up to hang with the fam."

"Ivy?"

"International student," she sang, doing a little dance. "Flights are crazy expensive and my parents understand I'm trying to save money. So, when Lindsay leaves me on Christmas, I'll just run around the place naked, singing carols at the top of my lungs."

"I hope not." Jade walked in, cutting into our laughter. "I'll still be here, Ivy. Yes to singing Christmas carols. No to running around naked."

Ivy snapped her fingers. "Shit. There goes my holiday."

"We can plan to do something together," I said. "Just us leftover Zetas."

"That would be great. Thank you."

"Of course. I wouldn't leave my sisters sitting alone in an empty house during the holidays."

"I'll be alone in an empty house," Sofia piped up. She leaned far back from the counter as she chopped the onions. "My parents are doing renovations on the house and going to Jamaica to escape them. They offered to pay for me to go with them, and I ended up deciding to stay and get some work done."

I gave her a crazy look. *Jamaica? Renovations? What is she talking about?*

"Are you staying at Val's place?" Lindsay asked.

"Nah, I'll be here with you guys. We can go out, see the lights, and do some Christmas shopping." Sofia flashed me a half smile. "Sorry, Val, I know you said I can stay, but you're a family of seven and I'd hate to impose. You'll come over and stay with me a few nights, won't you?"

My jaw worked. I studied Sofia, fighting to figure out what she wanted me to say. "Um... yes?"

"Awesome." She clapped. "We'll have our own little celebration before everyone breaks up. We'll pick a night to make cookies, decorate a tree, wrap gifts, and watch Christmas movies. Val, you can sleep over."

Understanding dawned on me. "Sure. That sounds perfect. What do you think, ladies?"

"I'm in."

"Yes, please."

"I would love to join too." Jade settled at the dining table with her laptop. "If that's okay, Valentina?"

I stretched my smile as far as it could go. "It's okay with me as long as by then you've told me everything you know about Maverick's disappearance."

"That's easy," she rebounded. "I don't know a thing. How can I prove it to you?"

"You can't. I guess I'll just not trust you until Maverick comes back and tells me otherwise."

"I'm sorry to hear that."

"I bet you are," I muttered under my breath, thinking of the conversation Ryder and Ezra overheard. This woman could play the "I'm innocent" violin better than a maestro.

"Let's talk about something else," Lindsay said. "Val, you have a son. What are you getting him for Christmas?"

"What do you get the boy who has everything?" I tossed my head, grinning. "He's on a giraffe kick right now. We're planning a trip to the zoo. It'd make his whole year to get a picture with one. It's also his birthday coming up, so I have to ration out the excitement."

"Ugh. I'm in the same boat," Ivy said. She chopped the garlic up fine and handed it to me. "My birthday is a week after New Year's. By then, everyone's broke from Christmas and I had to make do with the gifts I already got. Can't complain though. Mom and Dad still found a way to make my birthday special."

I side-hugged her. "Your sisters will too."

"Any excuse to stuff our face with cake," Lindsay agreed.

"Thanks, guys."

"After Christmas, we'll have a sisters' day," Sofia said. She nodded imperceptibly at me, and again I flailed wondering what she wanted me to say next. "Mani-pedis, lunch somewhere fancy, and shopping. Val and I will split the cost. It'll be our gift to you."

Ivy ducked her head. "You don't have to do all that."

"Val," Jade sliced in.

Sofia's hands disappeared under the counter.

"We have a birthday fund to celebrate each sister," Jade continued. "It allows for seventy-five dollars each to buy cakes, decorations, and the rest. There's no need for you to come out of pocket for Ivy's birthday."

"I wasn't thinking about the standard school-year parties, Jade. Ivy's here without her friends, family, and most of the Zetas are gone. I figured we could do better than a Publix cake and dollar store streamers for five people."

My phone buzzed. I checked it discreetly.

Sofia: Suggest a mall we could go to. Snow Valley or Knightons.

"It's truly no problem, Ivy. I'd die for a girls' day grabbing lunch at De Presco's, and shopping at Knightons."

"Oh no, Val," Sofia piped up. "We can't do Knightons. Didn't you hear?"

"Hear what?"

"They've been having problems with pickpockets lately. They think it's teenagers blending in, coming up behind people while they're shopping, eating, or walking around. They don't notice their wallets or phone is gone till it's too late."

"And who notices one particular group of teenagers among hundreds," Lindsay added. "I bet they're no closer to catching them."

"They're not," Sofia replied. "I'm going to sound like such an old lady, but when I was a teenager, the most dangerous thing I did was sneak out of the dorms to see my boyfriend."

I laughed. "Doesn't sound that wild, but trust me, at our school that was grounds for expulsion," I told Ivy and Lindsay. "Sofia lived life on the edge. I was the goody-two-shoes."

"You were also a mom," Lindsay said. "You had to grow up faster than us." She heaved a sigh. "While I took full advantage of my wild teen years."

"Uh-oh," I cried. "Are we talking a few five-finger discounts?"

Screwing up her face, she squealed as she nodded.

"Bad girl!" Sofia smacked her bottom. "What about you, Ivy? Are you joining our ranks?"

"I'm leading the ranks. I invented rebellion, ladies. We're talking sneaking out every night, dating all the guys my mom told me to run from, and a tagging-cop-cars phase."

We hooted and hollered.

"You win," I said. "We bow to you."

We bowed and scraped, cracking her up.

"What about you, Jade?" Sofia asked. "One of the good girls or the bad?"

She looked up from her laptop like she was surprised we were talking to her. "I'm not sure how appropriate this is."

I groaned. "Jade, you say you're here as part of the family, and you have no other motive than to support us, but every time we try to draw you in, you act like our drill sergeant and we're cadets who must observe protocol at all times. And you wonder why I'm suspicious of you?"

Jade tensed.

"Why can't you joke around and have fun with us for once?"

My challenge hung heavy in the air. As crushing as the silence. Finally, I knew what Sofia was trying to do, and I wasn't letting Jade wiggle out without a fight.

"Valentina," she began. "You're right."

I blinked. *I am?*

"Lately, I have behaved more as a drill sergeant than a housemother. The way I've been on you girls to meet your requirements, I know it's eroding away the comfort I wanted you all to have with me. I apologize," she said, standing up. "Running the sorority is your job, and from now on, I will let you do it, Valentina."

"Thank you."

She smiled. "I admit though, I'm not as comfortable talking about my past. I did a lot of things I'm not proud of. But I turned it around when I came to Somerset and joined the sorority. I will say this: Zeta Rho saved me.

"This house. The women I befriended. The demands put on me to work harder and strive further. I wouldn't be who I am today without this place. Whoever you were in high school is not who you have to be." She squeezed Ivy's shoulder. "You have dozens of sisters behind you now."

She took her laptop and left us. I put myself to the task of cooking, laughing and joking with the girls like it was all fine, while my thoughts ran a mile a minute.

Sofia and I shared a look over the saucepot. If we thought our subtle questioning would reveal the truth about Jade, we were wrong. She walked away leaving behind more questions.

After lunch, Sofia walked me to my car.

"What do you think? Doing things she wasn't proud of? Turning her life around?" she repeated. "That's the kind of heavy regret that'd come from driving a girl to commit suicide."

"I agree. Didn't sound like she just had a few petty thefts in her background. I'm not saying you wouldn't feel guilty about that if you did change your life, but it sounded like Adult Jade did a one-eighty from Teen Jade, and she's not eager to relive those years."

Sofia opened my door for me. "We can't be sure, of course. She might not be the thief or the bully and have something else entirely to atone for. It's a place to start, though, when we question her and get the fucking truth."

"I'm compelled to say this doesn't have to be *we*, Sofia. This is my problem, not yours. You don't have to get dragged into whatever crazy shit is going on."

"Val, for a smart girl, you say some dumb crap when you're ready."

I barked a laugh.

"I've known Maverick since preschool. Things got rough in high school, but when he got his head out of his ass and treated you like the queen you are, we patched up and became friends for real. I want him home too, Val. I'll do whatever I can to help you."

"Thanks, Sof." I hugged the stuffing out of her. "I could not hold it together without you. I'm serious. The guys would have to scrape me out of bed every day. You keep me sane."

She popped a kiss on my cheek. "You were there for me every time I fell apart. This is what we do, Val, we're a team."

"What now?" I asked softly. "You've pretty much been running this show. Give me my orders."

"I'll plan our girls' night for next weekend," she said. "Jade's pretty much confirmed she'll be here the entire break, so she'll be hanging around that night. When her guard is down and everyone's sleeping, we make it clear she'll lose this sorority she loves so much if she doesn't tell us everything she knows about Maverick."

"Got it. I'm in."

"Should we tell Ryder, Ezra, and Jaxson?"

"I promised them no secrets, but if I flood the house with my boyfriends next weekend, she'll know something is up."

"They'll have to trust we can handle this ourselves."

I snorted. "They'll show their trust by hiding outside in the shadows, ready to run in at a loud sneeze."

"Might not be a bad thing. Not saying I'm going to back out, because I'm committed to the plan, but Jade looks like she can take us."

"Not gonna lie. I'm pretty sure she can too."

Aiden pushed open the fence, carrying a bag of leftover barbecue trash. Our eyes locked across the lawn.

"My guys will do what they have to do, and I'll do what I have to do," I said without breaking our gaze. "Bye, Sof. I'll see you next weekend if not before."

She followed my sight. "I know what you're thinking. Do you really want to have it out right here on the lawn?"

"Better than alone in the woods. At least there are witnesses in case he tries to drown me in the birdbath."

"I'll be right here."

Nodding, I gave her one last hug and approached Aiden. He dumped the trash—his face expressionless as he dusted off his hands.

"Aiden."

"Moon," he said.

No, not expressionless. There was a tightness to his jaw and a crinkle around his left eye that said pissed.

"Something I can do for you?"

"I've been wanting to talk to you for a while, but I figured you had something to say to me first."

"Like what?"

I lifted my shoulders. "How about an apology?"

Aiden scoffed. "Are you serious? You stalked me, harassed my parents, chased me through the street, and you expect me to apologize? You really are delusion—"

I socked him dead in the mouth.

Aiden crashed over the garbage bins. "Bitch! What the fuck?!"

"The apology was for hitting and throwing me in a lake. I can't swim, jackass. The punch was for calling me delusional," I said. "I'm not hearing that anymore. I know you're up to your shriveled balls in Maverick's disappearance."

He kicked the bins off him, scrambling up. A dab of blood decorated the corner of his mouth.

"I don't know anything!"

"So you ran away from me because what? You were embarrassed by your mom's tea cozies? For once, Aiden. For ten fucking seconds. Stop lying."

"You want the truth?" he hissed. Aiden got in my face. "The truth is you're in way over your head and have no idea who you're messing with.

And no matter how much you try to goad me. Or how many bugs you leave in my apartment."

Surprise rocked me off my feet.

"You will never know the truth, Moon. Despite what Leighton told you, you're not cut out for this. You becoming a Zeta was a mistake. You don't belong here, and you never will. Now go back to playing house with your kiddie and fifty boyfriends. You're not worth my time."

Aiden turned his back on me. I watched him storm off in a strange mood. One I didn't identify till I was in my car and halfway home.

It wasn't the bullshit he said about not belonging in Zeta Rho. It wasn't the crack about Leighton, or the knowledge she shared about how much she wanted me in the sorority. It was that no matter what I did, I couldn't break through the wall around Aiden Connelly.

Questioning his parents didn't work. Throwing the truth in his face didn't work. Punching and busting his lip didn't work. He would not be brought down by anger, truth, or lies.

There was nothing for it. If I was going to tear down those walls and get through to Aiden, I'd have to do things that haven't yet occurred to me. Commit acts I never thought myself capable of.

Aiden knew where Maverick was. Deep in my soul, I knew he did.

The gloves were off now. Aiden's time was up.

I SKIRTED OVERACTIVE seven-year-olds, picking up fallen cups and licked-clean paper plates. My companion hung off my neck in total bliss—content to be out of her cage and seeing the world.

I assumed. Who knows what a snake is thinking?

Jaxson cut me off coming out of the kitchen. "Sorry, bab— Fuck!" He jumped back ten feet. "What are you doing with that thing?"

Giggles sounded from the patio entrance. Three little munchkins stuck their heads inside. "Fuck!" they crowed.

"Jaxson!"

"I said fudge," he shouted.

They ran away laughing their heads off.

"Nicely done, babe." He gave me and my legless friend a wide berth as I made for the trash. "Their parents will never let them come back here. They always give me side-eye for being twenty-one with a seven-year-old."

"They can shove their side-eye back up their... bottom," he finished at my look. "Besides, we don't want those three mini-demons back. I caught them literally climbing the walls. Demon One was halfway off the drape preparing to leap onto the blanket Demon Two and Demon Three were holding out."

"Yikes," I said between giggles. "Caroline was right. We should've kept the party outside so we wouldn't have all these kids running free in this big mansion."

"We tried, but Adam had to show them his jungle room, and once they were in— Dammit, Val. I can't talk to you while you're wearing that thing."

"This sweet lady? She's just a little python," I crooned, stroking her scales. "Since when are you afraid of snakes?"

He visibly shuddered. "What rational person likes snakes?"

"Alright, alright." I stuck my head outside.

Adam's party was in full swing. We decided to skip the event planner and handle everything ourselves. We killed it—if I say so myself.

We set up tables throughout the lawn covered in animal plates, animal balloons, and stuffed critters for each kid to take home. The big balloon guy came early that morning to inflate the life-sized rhino, giraffe, elephant, and the rest. We had a fleet of toy Jeeps the children rode to weave through the animals. All that on top of the four separate live animal shows featuring snakes, lemurs, petting zoo, and bunnies, Adam was having so much fun, he was almost distracted from missing Maverick.

Almost.

I headed off a meltdown that morning by promising we'd record every second of his party, and when Maverick came back, they'd watch it together and Adam could tell him what happened. It made Adam feel better, but not me. I promised I'd have him home by now. All these weeks later, I was still playing the "what are you talking about?" game with Aiden and Jade.

I passed the snake off to her handler, then enfolded myself in Jaxson's arms.

"I know," he said gently. "I know."

"If you know, then the three of you will stop fighting me. I have to confront Jade. This has gone on long enough."

"You don't have anything to confront her with. You've got spilled secrets with no name to put them to. You've got a vague comment about turning her life around. What happens when you threaten to get her removed for driving a kid to suicide, and she has no idea what you're talking about?

"Not only will you give away that you've been digging in her life too, but she'll have grounds to get rid of *you*. Jumping and blackmailing your housemother sounds like an expulsion-worthy offense to me."

"I know the risks. I also know it's long past time to accept them. If I don't do everything I can to get him back, I'll never forgive myself. Being able to look you, myself, and our son in the eye is more important than Somerset or Zeta Rho."

"We're not going to talk you out of this, are we?"

I smiled up at him. "I'm afraid not."

"Fine. But you're not going to be alone. Pull the same trick as Connelly. Keep your phone on the whole time. If we hear things going wrong, we'll bust in."

"How did I know you were going to say that?"

"You probably knew I was going to say this too: bring your Taser. Drop that woman if she even thinks of making a sudden move."

"I have no problem agreeing to that condition. Sofia and I are fairly sure Jade can take us."

He groaned, dropping his head. "Is that supposed to make me feel better about this?"

"Sorry, I take it back. What I meant is Jade has two noodle arms and a cotton-candy backside. She'll drop if we blow too hard on her."

"Cotton-candy backside?" He laughed. "What is that?"

"You know. Light, soft, barely there."

"Damn, it's crazy how much I love you."

"Not that crazy," I said between kisses. "It's how much I love you."

THAT NIGHT, I TUCKED Adam into bed, counting kisses on his face for his new age.

"—five, six, seven!" we cried.

Adam squirmed under his covers, giggling. "I had the best birthday ever."

"I know. We made every family in the neighborhood jealous. They're going to have a hard time topping that."

"Yeah!"

Adam reached under the sheets and tugged the lump out. My brows wrinkled on the stuffed giraffe that was not Tim. Looking around, I spotted his old best friend tucked in the mound of toys by his reading nook.

"What's this, baby? Where did you get him?"

"Her name is Alba. Daddy gave her to me."

"Aw. Such a nice present." I tucked them both in tight. "Adam, I'm sorry Daddy Maverick couldn't come to your birthday p-party." My voice cracked, and I tried to cover it. "He really wanted to be there."

"It's okay, Mommy. I know Daddy has to work."

"Yes," I said, seizing on the excuse. "He has a lot going on right now, but nothing is more important than you. He'll be home soon."

"Okay. Good night." He flipped over, eyes falling shut.

"Do you want me to stay with you till you fall asleep?"

"No. I'm too big for that now," he said, crushing my heart in that matter-of-fact way children perfect. "Wake me up early, Mom. Daddy and I have work tomorrow."

By work, he undoubtedly meant Ryder was going into the office to manage the global construction company saddled on his shoulders, and Adam was going to follow behind him, looking cute and passing drawings to his favorite people. Seven years old and his future employees already loved him.

"How early are we talking?"

"Six."

"Hmm. How about I wake you at eight, we have a nice breakfast, and then I drive you into work to meet up with Dad?"

"Okay."

"You really are living the sweet life, Adam Moon."

He tittered like someone who knew, but wasn't going to say anything.

"A kiss good night for you." I pecked his forehead. "And a kiss good night for Alba. Love you."

"Love you too."

After shutting Adam's door, I squared my shoulders. The guys were waiting up for me.

Jaxson and I ended the conversation about Jade on such a high note. It gave me a false sense of optimism going into my arguments with Ezra and Ryder. They were not so easily swayed, and I left for Zeta Rho the following week, arguing with them all the way to the car.

"We're following you, Val," Ezra said. He unlocked his car to prove it. "You know we're not letting you go alone."

"Come, then. Hide in all the bushes you want. But the point is to catch her off guard. If she thinks something is up, what's to stop her walking out the door and driving off. She doesn't have to be in the Zeta house. It's winter break."

"Keep your phone on," Ryder said.

"I've told you twenty times that I will."

"Good. While you're being so agreeable, stay home and let us handle this."

"I'm not staying home. I'm not fighting about this anymore. And I'm not going to be late," I said. "We'll be going till Ivy, Lindsay, and Jade fall asleep. It'll be early in the morning. If you want to be close by, wait till I call you. I don't want you trapped in your cars till three a.m."

"We'll be fine, Val," Ryder said. "Just—"

"—keep my phone on," I finished. "Got it."

The guys finally let me go. I played music during the drive to both psych myself up and calm down. I knew what I had to do and was as ready as I'd ever be to do it. Jade Ortega would tell me the truth that night. I wouldn't give her another choice.

The ladies were in the kitchen baking cookies in their pajamas when I arrived—Jade included.

"Smells amazing in here," I said. "What are you making?"

"Chocolate sugar cookies, gingerbread cookies, shortbread cookies, and the big daddy, an eggnog cheesecake," said Sofia. "We all picked a recipe and went for it. What do you got for us?"

I showed off my Tupperware. "I shook things up and made peanut brittle. Who's got the movies?"

"Me," said Ivy. "All the classics."

"Is the living room set up? Do you need me to do that?"

"Already done," Lindsay said. "Just the tree left to decorate."

"Perfect. Can I put the music on?" I asked.

"I've got that." Jade abandoned her batter and went into the room. We set up a system that played music on the speakers throughout the house. A splurge I'm glad I talked Blair into.

"Someone give me a whisk," I said.

"To help?" Ivy asked.

"To eat."

The night was so much fun, it was easy to pull myself out of dark thoughts and enjoy singing, dancing, and decorating the tree with the girls. Jade didn't hang around too much. She helped with the baking and joined us for one movie. After, she went upstairs to Skype her family.

Sofia and I curled up in our sleeping bags. The living room was a Christmas wonderland. Ivy, Lindsay, and Sofia hung white fairy lights around the wall and on the couches. Frosted snowflakes were taped to the wall, and stockings with our names on them hung off the television stand. This wasn't just about Jade. I wanted to have this time with Sofia and the sisters who stayed behind. It was times like this I found my pockets of normal.

Multicolored lights cast blue, red, green, and yellow over the cookies placed between us. Sofia and I shared a plate, and the same thoughts, while *Elf* made us laugh for the sixth time.

"When?" Sofia whispered.

"When they fall asleep."

She nodded. No more was said.

Ivy passed out during *Grinch*. Lindsay was next to go five minutes into *The Christmas Carol*.

I raised my head, checking to make sure they were out.

"Let's give it twenty minutes," I said, shutting off the television. "Make sure the house is quiet."

No answer.

I looked over at Sofia. She was dead asleep.

Biting back a grin, I burrowed into my pillow to wait those twenty minutes. Let her get a catnap. I'd wake her and call the guys when it's time.

Wherever you are, Maverick, I'm coming for you. Just keep fighting. I'm coming.

"... sleep..."

My eyes flew open.

Soft footfalls sounded in the hall. Jade was clearly still awake.

The living room doors creaked open.

I squeezed my eyes shut. She was probably checking to see if we were sleeping. Once she backed out and went up to bed, I'd do what I came here to do.

I sensed a presence over me.

Go back to bed, Jade. This will all be—

A hand clamped over my mouth.

"Shh." Hot breath poured in my ear. "Don't make a sound, Moon."

That was not Jade.

"We need to have a little talk. Come with us."

Aiden hauled me up. Thinking quick, I flashed out and kicked Sofia's shoulder. She moved but didn't wake, and my last chance was gone.

Aiden dragged me into the hallway. A figure stood cloaked in shadows—concealing all but the wide, satisfied smirk twisting her lips.

"Upstairs," hissed Jade. "Let's get this over with."

I clawed at Aiden's hand, straining to tear it off my face. A sharp pain ripped through my ear.

"Hmm!" *He bit me? The fucker bit me!*

"Enough."

On the contrary. It wasn't enough. I kicked, flailed, clawed, and earned myself another bite on the ear. Harder the second time. Wetness dripped down my neck.

The two of them carried me upstairs and into her room. One look and I realized while Sofia and I were plotting, Aiden and Jade were too. We weren't the only ones who saw the opportunity in this sleepover.

A lone chair sat in the middle of the room. The two of them forced me into it. Aiden shoved my hands through the zip ties and pulled tight. I couldn't scream. Jade had long since shoved the kitchen dishcloth into my mouth. Bound, gagged, and bleeding, my first thought—first emotion wasn't fear as they stood back and admired their handiwork. My first thought... was of Maverick.

Was this how they got him? Attacked while he thought he was safe talking to a friend? Tied him up? Gagged him?

Hurt him?

No, I wasn't scared.

Thick, seeping, corrosive anger flushed out all thoughts and emotions, breaking something inside me. I couldn't tell you what I made up my mind to do next. It wasn't a conscious thought. All I knew was what reflected in their eyes, echoed in my soul. This ends tonight.

"I'm sorry it's come to this, Valentina," Jade began. "It wouldn't have had to, but you refuse to let this go. Stalking. Harassing Aiden's parents. Attacking him."

"We'll say this one last time," Aiden said. "We don't know where your boyfriend is. We had nothing to do with his disappearance. If you come near my family or threaten me again, I'll take out a restraining order. The bugs I found in my apartment will easily convince a judge you're dangerous. May even convince the dean that you don't belong here at all. It'll be hard to run the house next door when you have to stay a thousand feet away."

I lifted my chin—unable to speak, but having nothing to say even if I could. Their threats did not reach me.

"Val, the mistrust and disharmony in this house has gone on long enough," said Jade. "If it continues, I will go to Mrs. Kessler and have you removed as president. Yes, she can do so. If she decides you're wrong for Zeta Rho, a two-thirds vote from the sisters can be overridden." Jade patted my arm, making my skin crawl. "Nod if you understand and agree to leave this nonsense behind us."

I nodded.

"Excellent, Valentina. I'm so glad you're finally willing to be reasonable."

The cloth stretched my jaw to break. I was losing feeling in my fingers, but at least we were all willing to be reasonable.

"Hmm hmm mm."

"I'll remove the gag," she said, slowly approaching. "I would not recommend screaming."

I nodded again.

Jade tugged it out, and didn't go far. She hovered over me ready to stuff it back in if my voice squeaked higher than a mouse.

I cleared my throat—calm and collected as I took them both in.

"Is that it?" I asked. "Restraining orders and losing my presidency? That's all you got to talk me into abandoning my boyfriend? That's a joke, right?" My gaze flicked over their shoulder to the door.

"Actually, no," Aiden said. "We had more but you agreed so quickly."

I fixed on him and his grin.

"I see you need the whole speech."

"Lay it on me."

"Fine." Aiden clutched my arms, bending to stick his face in mine. "If you don't back off, it won't just be you we take down. A few bands will remember they've got grounds for a lawsuit against Jaxson Van Zandt that'll bring Interstellar Records to their knees. Your boy, Ezra, got himself shot and then had to send Mommy to take care of the mess her boys made with the Sons of Slaughter.

"I hear they're convinced they've wiped out the whole gang, but there's always someone left. Someone who cut a deal to get out of a long sentence. Someone who got a long sentence and is inside counting the days. Or someone who watched their dad or husband get carted off to jail and wants revenge. Any one of them would take a free ticket to Evergreen and put it to good use making sure your loveable snitch tells the rest of his secrets to God."

I dug my nails in the chair, barely feeling the pain of them bending back.

"As for Ryder Shea. He's a hard man to get to since he's surrounded by his security. Especially his trusty sidekick, Jacob. But every man has his weakness, and Shea's happens to be his sweet old mom."

My eyes hardened. "Careful, Connelly."

He laughed. "What? I'm not going to hurt her. I don't have to. She's given the world the perfect blackmail and everyone's either been too oblivious to see it, or they were silenced."

"What the hell are you talking about?"

"Ryder isn't Benjamin Shea's son."

I froze. Time froze.

What did he say?

"Excuse me? Where did you—?"

"Save it. You're a smart girl who has been living in their home and flipping through the family albums longer than I have. Don't tell me you didn't notice Caroline and Benjamin have widow's peaks, but Ryder does not. Ryder has a pronounced jaw while Daddy Ben barely had a chin. Ryder has the rarest eye color on earth, while both his parents have standard issue like most of the population. You can't deny his relation to Caroline, but he looks nothing—*nothing* like Benjamin... and that's not something Caroline Shea wants the world to know."

I got in his face. "You don't know what the hell you're talking about. You sound so stupid right now. The only reason I'm not laughing my ass off is because I'm not looking to be gagged again."

Aiden's grin widened. "I struck a nerve. If I didn't have proof before, I have it now. Ryder isn't a Shea. What will the shareholders think when they find out the company was taken over by a bastard? Their family will be dragged through the press all over again. What will Ms. Caroline do to prevent that from happening? I bet she won't risk her son to save another."

"Let me out of these. Now."

"You can go at any time, Valentina," Jade said. "As long as we understand each other. This matter is dropped. Stop questioning us about your boyfriend's disappearance. Let the police do their work. I'm sure they'll find him safe and sound soon enough."

"Let me out now."

"Say you'll drop it," Aiden said. "Don't sacrifice three boyfriends for one."

I blinked at him. "I'm not going to tell you again."

"Listen, b—"

The door flew open. Jaxson and Ezra were on them as they spun. Aiden didn't get a chance to get his hands up. Fifty thousand volts surged through their bodies, dropping both flat on their asses.

They didn't get up.

"Val, are you okay?" Sofia threw her arms around me. She drew back, eyes widening at the blood staining her cheek and mine. "Val!"

"I'm okay," I rushed out. "It barely hurts. Nothing a rabies shot won't take care of."

"I'm so sorry," Sofia said. "I fell asleep."

Ryder stalked around the room looking for something to cut me out.

"When I woke and found you gone, I crept upstairs to see if you were doing it without me and…"

"Sof, it's not your fault. It turned out they had the same ambush plan that we did. They just got to theirs first."

Ryder snatched the scissors from the bedside dresser drawer. I fell into their hug.

"I'm okay, guys, I swear." I kissed Ryder's cheek. "How much of that did you hear?"

"We heard enough," Ezra said. "Play along, or they'll blow up our lives."

I turned on them, sensing that odd feeling grip me. "Ryder, did you find more of those zip ties while you were searching?"

"In the desk." There was a blank note in his voice I rarely heard from him. He heard what Aiden said all right. They knew he wasn't

Benjamin Shea's son, and they were willing to blackmail his recovering mother to stop him searching for our family.

I didn't know what would happen to Jade and Aiden that night. There's a light that goes off in someone's eyes when they reach the point of no return. An acceptance that from this moment forward, the person you are is left behind, and a new person capable of horrible acts you can't yet comprehend will move forward.

I saw the look for the first time in the mirror over the sink as I washed the dishes, tucking a soapy knife in my pocket. I saw it again in the eyes of Ryder, Ezra, Jaxson, and Sofia. I knew without looking what was in mine.

"Get them," I said calmly. "My conversation with Aiden and Jade is far from over."

We moved in silence, carrying Aiden to the desk to bind his arm to the leg. Jade was placed in the chair she so kindly set out for me. She stirred as the zips were tightened around her wrists.

"Give me a minute." I went down, rescued the bag I left tucked beside the living room couch, confirmed Lindsay and Ivy were still dead to the world, and returned to the bedroom.

Jade's eyes were fluttering open. Just in time.

"Jade." I shut and locked the door behind me. "Wake up."

"What...?" she muttered. "What happened?"

"Baby," I said, stroking that prominent jaw I was glad set him apart from Benjamin. "Let me do this, please. I promise these two will regret their little threats and walk out of here groveling."

Jade's vision cleared on me.

"That's if they want to walk out of here at all."

Jade snapped around, seeing Aiden. She bucked in the chair, hands straining against the plastic, and nearly tipped herself back. Jaxson caught and set her upright. The gag was stuffed in her mouth the second she opened it to scream.

"What are you thinking, Jade? You shout the place down, Lindsay and Ivy will come running, then you'll have witnesses backing up that I'm dangerous and unstable the next time you blackmail me into letting you get away with kidnapping my boyfriend?" I sat on the edge of her bed, folding my legs.

"Good plan. Honestly, all of this was well thought out. If I was any other woman, your threats wouldn't have worked because—people who love someone don't give up that easily—but it would've scared me into moving quietly and cautiously against you.

"The problem is, you didn't tie those women to a chair. You threatened me."

Jade's eyes narrowed. Fury like I'd never seen poured from her gaze and burned me inside out.

"Did you ever find out what was written on the card Leighton gave me that night?" I asked. "I don't know how high this goes, or how it works in your little kidnapping club, but I'm starting to get now that the initiation is important. It's all a part of keeping the Zetas and Alphas slightly off-balance and constantly afraid.

"But my card, it didn't have anything about dads with second families or affairs with my teacher. My secret is... I'm a murderer."

Jade's eyes twitched—a quick widening that I would've missed if I wasn't trained on her. She didn't know my secret.

"I killed a man to protect someone I love," I continued, voice steady. "It's an act that haunts me to this day, but if I had to go back and do it over again, I would. Leighton thought that made me the perfect sister for Zeta Rho Sigma. Leighton did not understand me, and neither do the two of you."

Aiden pulled a face. He was beginning to wake.

"A woman who would kill for the person they love isn't fazed by your tricks. Don't get me wrong, I'm sure you have every intention of carrying out your threats, but *it won't stop me*," I said, leaning in. "Nothing you do will stop me, Jade. Nothing I do will be too much. If you don't tell me where Maverick is, I— Well, I will have to hurt you."

I shrugged. "In as many ways as I can think of until you tell me what I need to know. Nod if you understand."

Jade didn't move.

I held the stun gun to her knee and set it off.

"Hmmm!" Jade screamed through the gag, her body jerking and seizing.

I turned the power down so she wouldn't pass out again. At this level, it just hurt like a bitch.

Getting up, I circled her. Jade huffed and puffed through the gag. Ezra stuffed one in Aiden's mouth, catching him while he was groggy and fighting to peel his eyes open.

"You two weren't the only ones digging into other people's business," I said. "I know all about you, Jade, and Sylvie Marin."

Jade's jaw went slack. I helped her out by tugging free the cloth.

"How?" she rasped. Her skin washed out in the scant moonlight peeking through the curtains.

Jade's bedroom was a classy, serene place filled with yoga mats, exercise equipment, candles, pleasing colors, self-help books, and half-burned sticks of incense. I figured it out before Jacob called and confirmed a girl committed suicide in Jade's old high school. She was someone desperate to find inner peace.

"I know bullies, Jade." I traced a line between her eyes. "People like you wear the mark in the curve of your scowl and the judgment in your eyes. You never escaped that cruel, vicious girl who relentlessly hounded an innocent person—"

"Innocent?!" Jade shrieked. "You don't know what happened. You don't know a thing! I didn't want her to die, but Sylvie was *far* from innocent."

"See?" I hissed in her ear. "This is the real you, Jade. The one still riding the high of justice served against someone too weak to fight you off."

"No. That's not me anymore. I regret what I did. I've changed."

"Into what exactly? Is the woman who's been lying, taunting, and tied me to a chair supposed to be better or worse than the girl you were in high school?"

"I didn't want to do this! We had to stop you—"

"Mhh!" Aiden rammed the desk. We couldn't make out what he was shouting through the gag, but the message was clear. *Jade, shut up.*

"What? Are you going to fall silent because Aiden's throwing a tantrum?"

Jade closed her mouth. I sensed her walls shoring up, quickly rebuilding in the wake of her childhood trauma smashing through.

"If I were you, I wouldn't worry about him. Aiden was bragging so much about the bugs he found in his apartment, it's obvious he didn't find the drugs."

Aiden gave me a wild look. "Hmm."

That time I had no issue translating what he said. "Yes, Aiden. Since Jacob already has access to your apartment, I asked him to leave a few presents around because you're a cold-ass bastard who got Ezra shot, threatened to have my brother-in-law killed, and you smirked at me every chance you got since Maverick disappeared. It's the deepest wish of my life to put you through even a fraction of the pain you've inflicted on me and my family. Getting you thrown in a jail cell where tweakers pass your ass around to numb the withdrawal, is a start."

Aiden tossed his head.

"I know what you're thinking," I continued. "*She's bluffing. I searched my whole apartment top to bottom and didn't find any drugs.* Smart guy like you, I'm sure you were thorough, checking all the places most people don't think to look." I crouched down beside him. "That's why I told Jacob to put them in the plant soil, old markers you keep in your desk, the box of laundry powder over the washing machine, and a few other places."

I returned his grin tenfold, widening as his skin paled. "You didn't check those places, did you, Aiden?"

He lunged and ran straight into my stun gun. Aiden dropped back, thudding against the desk to wake the whole house.

"As I was saying, the police are going to get a tip at exactly"—I made a show of checking my watch—"six o'clock this morning that golden boy Aiden Connelly has weapons, drugs, and thousands in cash stashed away in his apartment. By now I know your friends can get you out of almost anything, but whatever sway they hold over the police doesn't extend to Amelia Lennox.

"Trust me. She's more than happy to blast your fall from grace on every media outlet in existence. I'd like to see you smirk your way out of that, asshole."

I reclaimed my seat on Jade's bed. "So, here is how it's going to go. Aiden, you tell me where Maverick is or you become one of the biggest headlines in Somerset history. Or, Jade, you tell me where Maverick is and I won't smash my face into that wall, walk into the police station with the bruises on my wrist and bitten ear, and tell them you tied and beat me up. Once they hear about your history of bullying and torture on top of the tension between us the last few months, they'll have no issue arresting you for assault.

"And if for some reason they do." I held out my hands. "I'm rich. I'll buy a judge to lock you up for the maximum sentence. You've got the same deadline as Aiden. Tell me by six or tell the cops."

I looked between them. "This offer only goes to one of you, and it's the one whose spills where Maverick is first. The other one will be dropped in the shit they made for themselves. What do you say? Who is going first?"

Neither Jade nor Aiden moved a muscle.

"Ezra," I said.

We electrocuted them at the same time. Jade's and Aiden's screams stirred nothing in me. I suspected this night would be filed in the red-tinged memories that would cling to me for the rest of my life. But if it brought Maverick home to me, this memory would not be tinged with regret.

"Did I forget to mention that we won't be sitting in silence, staring at each other till six? The longer you make me wait, the longer I'll make you burn."

"You're sick," Jade rasped. "Look at you, Valentina. Look at what you've become." She jerked her head at the wall mirror. "You're right. It's easy to spot a bully."

"Stop wasting my time." I gestured to Jaxson who put the gag back in. "We're not exchanging insults. The next thing out of your mouths will be Maverick's location. Nod when you're ready."

If I thought electric shock and jail sentences would loosen their tongues, I underestimated their stubbornness.

The sounds of Aiden's smothered cries faded. He was pouring buckets of sweat. His skin was flushed and haggard. That chiseled, handsome face looked like it aged ten years in one hour.

The hour had been no less kind to Jade. Her eyes were dropping. Head lolling as though her body had long since lost the ability to hold her up. It was her mental strength keeping her from the breaking point, and by the streaks running down her cheeks, it was about to lose the battle.

"Hmm mm hm."

"Ryder," I said. "Remove the gag, please."

Aiden shouted something we couldn't hear, clearly trying to warn Jade to keep her mouth shut.

"Why... are you doing this?" Jade's voice scraped from her throat. "You don't understand. It doesn't... have to be this way."

I considered her. "Why? Why doesn't it have to be this way?"

"We're not doing this because we want to. I'm not trying to hurt anyone, Valentina. I swear to you," she whispered. "I've changed. Everything I do now is to help."

"You've changed? How have you changed, Jade? I brought up your past and you rushed in with a justification, and then remembered you're supposed to feel remorse. Why wasn't Sylvie Marin innocent?"

"Because she killed my cousin."

My lips turned down at the corners. Sofia backed away from Jade, sharing my expression. The bed dipped as she sat next to me.

"What does that mean?" Sofia asked.

"It means what I just said. Sylvie Marin got blind drunk and mowed my cousin down in the street while she was walking up to the same party Sylvie was leaving." Tears ran hot and fast down her cheeks. "Sylvie's parents bought her out of trouble. By the end of the hearing, her lawyers had them all believing Maya caused her own death by walking in the street.

"Sylvie thought she could just come back to school like nothing happened. But... I couldn't let it g-go. She left Maya twisted and broken in the dirt. I wouldn't move on, and neither would she."

"So, you reminded her every single day of what she'd done," I said. There wasn't a trace of judgment in my tone. I couldn't approve of how Jade got her revenge. Still, if someone I love was taken in such a stupid, thoughtless, tragic way, there was every certainty I would do something I wouldn't approve of too.

"*Murderer* spray-painted on her locker and car. Shoving and knocking her down in the halls. Screaming her out of the cafeteria. It went on and on and on until..."

I nodded. I understood.

"I didn't want her to do that. I swear," Jade said. "Since, I've let go of my anger and grief. It was poisoning me. Turning me into someone I didn't recognize. As hard as it may be for you to believe, I'm a different person now, Valentina, and I don't wish you or your family harm."

"If that's the case, tell me where Maverick is."

She shook her head. "Maverick told you where he is. Why won't you accept—?"

I straightened. "The voicemail. You know about the voicemail he left for his parents."

"How?" Ryder demanded.

"I know he's not the victim of some sinister plot," Jade said. Aiden sounded off in the corner. "You think you have to do this, but you don't."

"Because Maverick's going to come back on his own?" I flung. "He would've done that a long time ago if he had the option."

"Sawyer and Teagan came back." Jade's gaze drilled a hole in my head. "Accept that you don't have a clue about what's going on here."

"You accept that I'll happily let my ignorance toss you in jail."

"We did say the next thing out of her mouth had to be Maverick's location," Ryder said. "Love, if you're tired, I'm happy to take over for you." He tugged the Taser free of my grip. "Personally, I think we've been giving them too much recovery time between hits. I say we keep it on them till they either break, or their hearts give out."

Ryder approached her, curling Jade into her seat as she screeched for him to get away. He swerved and fisted Aiden's hair. "I'm starting to see this guy is in charge. You jumped when he called you and said it's time to take care of Val. You refuse to talk while he's sitting in this corner demanding you be quiet. Either you care about him enough to stop me, or I do shock him into cardiac arrest and you don't have to worry about obeying him."

Ryder turned the Taser on him. Aiden's body jerked back, his muscles contracting under the current.

"No! Stop!"

"You decide when it stops, Jade," I said.

"Don't do this," she cried. "I told you that you don't understand what's going on."

Ryder stopped—only to turn up the intensity. "I guess you don't care about him. That works because neither do I."

"Stop," Jade said, halting Ryder a millimeter from his neck. "A number. I have a number."

"Hmmm!" Aiden shouted.

Jade turned away from him. "Call the number," she whispered, "then let us go. No cops, no arrests, no threats."

"I didn't ask for a number," I said. "Tell me where you're holding Maverick."

"Just call the fucking number! When you do, it'll all make sense."

I studied her. Jade held my gaze unflinchingly despite her damp skin and wild hair. Slowly, I took out my phone.

"What is it?"

She rattled off the digits. I typed them in and pressed the phone to my ear. The call picked up on the second ring.

"Hello," I said. "Who is this?"

"Hey, Val."

My lips parted. Words caught on the tip of my tongue and didn't come out.

"I don't know how you got this number." He chuckled. "You're resourceful, so it's not a surprise you did. I won't waste time asking, and just tell you that I love and miss you."

"Maverick." I didn't recognize the strangled whisper as my voice. "How?"

"Maverick?" Jaxson repeated. The guys descended on me, sucking out the air around me, or that's just how it felt.

"I can't tell you how, Val, or where. I shouldn't even be talking to you right now, but this is my chance to say what I haven't been able to. Stop looking for me."

The command physically knocked me back.

"I'm not in danger. I don't need help. Let this go, please."

"Let it go? How can you say that to me? What is going on?!"

"I can't say," he replied, tone steady. "I wish I could. I love you. Kiss Adam and Alba for me."

"Maverick, no. Wait!"

The line went dead.

I called the number back. Again. And again. And again. It rang and rang itself to a robotic voice that repeated there wasn't a voicemail set up to receive messages. Hang up and try again.

Jaxson, Ezra, Ryder, and Sofia pelted me with questions. Aiden ranted through the gag. Noise pelted me on all sides. All I could do was hang up, and try again.

"There you are." Jade's voice broke through the fog. The spinning room settled and my eyes fixed on a smile I knew well. "I told you that you didn't understand what was going on here. I have grounds to expel all four of you from this school. Let us both out of here now, and we'll forget the whole thing."

I opened my mouth. "I—"

"Now," she barked.

"Let them out."

"But, Val," Jaxson began.

"It doesn't matter anymore." I walked out of the room.

"Nothing does."

Chapter Six

R*yder*

The three of us observed Valentina in the living room, sipping tea and staring off into space. She'd been like that since our ill-fated night in the sorority house. We'd been forced to let Aiden and Jade Ortega free with promises of mutually assured destruction if they told anyone what happened that night. Not that we understood ourselves.

"What do we do?" Jaxson asked. He fiddled with a garland wrapped around the banister.

Christmas had come to Shea Manor. Lights hung in every room. Mistletoe over the doorways. Glinting trees in the living room, kitchen, and drawing room—all loaded with presents for Adam. Mom went overboard with the decorations to cheer up Val.

Not that it did much good.

"What can we do?" Ezra spoke up. "She just found out she spent weeks crying, worrying, and torturing people to find a guy who doesn't want to be found. What the hell is Maverick into? Was Valentina right about this being the work of a cult? Did they suck Maverick in that easily?"

I shook my head. "I doubt there's anything easy about what's going on here. But Ortega was right about one thing, we don't have a fucking clue, and we never did. The Maverick we know wouldn't have left us worrying about him when a fucking phone call would tell us he's okay. There's more to this, and I assume the message is stay out of the way and wait for Maverick to come back on his own."

"What if he doesn't?" Jaxson asked.

The question charged the air.

"She's asking herself the same thing," Ezra said. "I guess now we know why she won't move."

"There's something else to think about other than our brother who decided to fuck off and become best friends with his captors."

I tensed before the rest was out of Jaxson's mouth.

"All that stuff Connelly said about your old man. Was that true?"

"I'm surprised it took you this long to ask."

"We thought he was bullshitting," Ezra said. "Coming up with stuff to scare Val away, but the more I think about it, it makes sense. You don't have a thing in common with Benjamin Shea."

I didn't look away from Valentina. "I noticed that a long time ago. He hasn't exactly been around the last eight years to do a DNA test. Whether he is or he isn't, it wasn't worth going to Mom with accusations."

"But now someone else knows," Ezra said. "Connelly said that night will be forgotten as long as neither of us goes near him again."

I bobbed my head. "Jacob told me he moved out of his apartment two days ago. He's serious about us being done fucking with him."

"Exactly," Jaxson said. "We can't plant coke and pills in the flower pots anymore. We'll lose our edge against him while he still has one on you. It may be time for that talk with Caroline."

"Connelly isn't going near my mother or Valentina. Moving to a new apartment means nothing when we go to the same school. He's smart enough to know that."

"Ryder—"

"Drop it," I sliced in. "It's been twenty-one years. My sperm donor can wait. Right now, the person I need to talk to is Valentina."

"We," Ezra corrected.

"Hold on." I stopped him on the steps. "Let me do this alone first. I think I know what to say."

"You know what to say to make Maverick disappearing and dodging our calls all right?"

I nodded.

"Go for it," Jaxson said. "I can't stand seeing her like this."

Valentina didn't react to my approach, though she must have heard me. She was packed under three blankets, faced away from the Christmas decorations. As I stood over her, I realized she wasn't staring at nothing. Her hand peeked out from under the blankets, clutching her phone.

"How many times have you called today?" I asked.

"Five."

I kissed her temple and lingered before pulling back. Val didn't react either.

"You were right about him."

"What?"

I moved around her, kneeling in her eyeline. "You said Maverick was out there somewhere—safe and unharmed. You were right. You said Jade and Aiden were liars holding back what they knew about his disappearance. You were right." I closed my hand over hers. "You said Maverick would never miss Adam's birthday and let our son down. You were right."

She scoffed. "No, he wouldn't miss the party. Instead, he sneaks home to give Adam a giraffe, make him promise not to tell he was there, and then ran off knowing we were all worried sick about him! What kind of person does that?!" she shouted. "I knew? I knew?! I didn't know anything, Ryder.

"I didn't know if he was alive. I hid away from you guys and cried every day for three weeks, because I didn't know if I'd ever see him again. And now I find out that he— he let me go through that." She tossed her head. "I don't know anything, Ryder. Least of all about Maverick."

"That's not true." Her doubts tried and failed to penetrate me. Val had been strong for everyone since this began. From Ezra's shooting to Maverick's disappearance, and now this. She needed us to be strong for her. "You do know him. Better than anyone. Better than us. Maverick loves you so fucking much, I'd say it's insane if I didn't feel exactly how he does."

I tipped her chin up to peer in her eyes. "So, as someone who knows him inside and out, and keeps his balls rolling around in your purse next to the lip gloss."

A ghost of a smile appeared on her lips.

"Tell me why Maverick would do this, Val. Because if he's going to hurt you, he'll have a damn good reason."

"We would," Ezra said, coming into the room with Jaxson. "And that reason is always that we're trying to protect you."

"How is he protecting me? This doesn't protect me."

Ezra knelt at her other side. "They could have threatened to hurt you. Said if he didn't go along with whatever the hell they're doing, you'd be the next one thrown in the back of a van."

Val sniffed, but didn't reply. She was listening.

"You're still stuck with Connelly, Ortega, and the other Sallys and Sams who might be smiling and making nice, while they wait for someone up high to say go."

"The fact is we walked out on Connelly and Ortega too early," I said. "We didn't get out of them why they took Maverick, Sawyer, or why all this shit started in the first place. As Ortega threw in our face, we don't know anything about what they're getting up to. But we do know Maverick. Tell us, Val."

"I... I don't know what to say. I don't know what to think," she confessed. "No, the Maverick I know wouldn't put me through this. I guess I have to accept I don't know him anymore."

I flicked her forehead.

"Hey!"

"Enough with that shit. You didn't give up on him when we were riding on no fucking hope. We're not giving up now. Think, Val."

"Of what?" She threw the blankets away, shoving off the couch. "What am I supposed to be thinking of other than this meaning we've been off base the whole time. Maverick did leave that message for his parents. At some level, he's choosing to be away from us because he came back for Adam's party without a problem."

"But if it's all so innocent, and he's coming and going whenever he wants," Jaxson said, "why not tell us? One thing is for sure, the message he left his parents is trash. He didn't leave because he was stressed. Stupid mug practically pissed rainbows every day, he was so happy about you, Adam, school, and his robot nerd friends."

"Well, even if Maverick lied about the reason he's staying gone, how can we say he doesn't have a choice in this after that call? He told me to stop looking for him. He said he... He said..." Val trailed off. A strange look scrunched her face.

"What?" I prompted. "What did he say?"

"He said to kiss Alba and Adam," she whispered. I wasn't certain if she was answering me or talking to herself.

"So?"

"He told me to kiss that stupid, damn giraffe he brought here without seeing me. Why wouldn't he see me?"

Jaxson lifted his shoulders. "Would've been too hard to leave again if he did."

"Yes!"

We jerked.

"Adam couldn't stop him leaving. Whereas I would've tackled his ass and chained him to the bed. Oh my goodness, guys," she cried, throwing up her hands. "You said it. Maverick's parents said it. Why wasn't I paying attention?"

"Baby, you need to catch us up," Jaxson said. "We're lost."

"Don't you see? Alba!"

Valentina ran off. We stumbled over each other following her.

"Still lost," Jaxson shouted after her.

"When we talked to Maverick's parents, they said the voicemail couldn't be faked because Maverick was wise enough to leave a clue if he was in trouble. Well, that message could've been scripted, but the night I called him, he couldn't have known it was coming," Val got out in a rush as she bolted upstairs.

"It was four in the morning. Jade finally cracked to save that shit Aiden. Maverick had to be careful, but this time, there was no one telling him what to say. So why of all things did he bring up the giraffe? Why let me know he came home and then left me without a word? He knew that would crush me and—" Val pulled up so fast we almost ran into her. She cupped my and Jaxson's cheeks. "—Maverick would never hurt me without a reason."

"The giraffe," Ezra breathed. "There's a message in the giraffe."

Adam, Caroline, and Cara jumped when we burst into his room. Yowling, the cat streaked under the bed.

"Mommy?" The two of them were surrounded by toys, a puppy, and a tiny giraffe harmlessly riding Adam's toy Jeep.

"Adam, baby." Val sat down and picked up Alba. "Tell me about when Daddy gave this to you."

He scrunched up his little face. "But I told you."

"I know, but this is very important. You said Daddy was hiding in the bushes?"

Adam giggled. "He was funny. Dad said he was a hunter searching for lions, so he had to hide, but he didn't forget about my birthday."

"Did Daddy give you a message to give to me?"

"No."

Val picked up the giraffe. "Did he say anything about Alba?"

"Alba is very special." He took it and held the stuffed animal tight to his chest. "I have to keep her safe."

"She is special," Val agreed. "You know, Ryder has a bunch of cute bow ties we can put on Alba. To dress her up for when you three go to work. Why don't we put some on her?"

"Cool!" Just like that, he handed it back.

"I'll be right back," Val said, leading the three of us out of the room. "I'll bring all his ties and we'll have a fashion show."

"Nicely done," Jaxson said.

"It will be if there's really a message hidden in his animal." She examined every inch of it, flipping it up, down, and around. "It must be inside."

"We can't cut up Adam's birthday present."

"No cutting," she said. "Look."

Val pointed out a seam in Alba's leg. I squinted.

"The thread," I said. "It's darker."

"Someone cut her leg open and sewed it closed. I bet I know who."

"Damn, this is all feeling very international men of mystery. Why would Maverick have to go through all of that?" Ezra asked. "Why couldn't he just come out and say *they're keeping me in an old farm shed. Come and get me?*"

Val prodded and squeezed the leg. "I think I feel something. I don't know why yet, Ezra, but we're about to find out."

An hour later, Val carefully sewed Alba's leg closed next to the SD card we freed from her grip. We were gathered in Maverick's room, hunched over his work desk.

"Ryder, grab a handful of ties and bring her back to Adam, please. He's about to come looking for us."

I knocked Jaxson's shoulder. "He can do that. Plug the card in."

"Fuck you. I need to see what's on it too."

"You think we're going to keep it a secret?"

"Who knows?" he returned. "Maverick's keeping secrets. Why can't you?"

Val huffed. "I'll go. Do not look without me."

She and Alba walked out, leaving us stuck. Of course we couldn't look at it without her.

We stood awkwardly around the desk, trying not to look at the card.

"Why'd it take us so long to find this?" Ezra moved to the couch. "Maverick should've told Adam to say he gave it to him."

"Adam *did* say Daddy gave it to him," Jaxson reminded. He threw himself down and kicked his feet up on the table. "It's our fault for all going by the same name. I vote I keep Dad. Ryder, you're Pops. Ezra, get used to Baba. It means *Dad* in Arabic."

"I know what it means."

"Pops is an eighty-year-old man with a potbelly and twelve grand-children," I said.

"How about Pappy? Old man? Dada?"

I stifled a snort. "Fuck off. Next time, we'll ask Adam which one."

It felt like hours we waited for Val to come back. In reality, it was twenty-seven minutes.

"Love, I'm afraid you have to say goodbye to your Gucci silk clover bow tie."

"Shit," I muttered. "Alba's got expensive taste."

"Did you look?"

"Not without you." I bounded across the room, phone already out. Val clutched my arm as I inserted the card. Her grip tightened with every passing second it took to go into the files and download the con-tents. Black swallowed the screen.

One second, two, three—

The lights turned on. Blinding white as brilliant as the sun. The camera spun, and then there was Maverick.

"Hey, Val."

Choking, she snatched the phone from me.

Maverick must have been playing hunter again. Branches stuck in his face and fallen leaves decorated his shoulder. Still, he looked fine.

There wasn't a scratch on him that I could see. But I did peek the smile on his face, looking through the lens at the woman he knew was on the other side.

"Man, I wish I could say this to you face-to-face. I wish I could see your face. Touch you. Hold you. Kiss you. They say the withdrawal period is the worst for addicts and they weren't kidding."

Val half laughed, half sobbed.

"There isn't time to say everything I need to." Maverick craned his neck. He appeared to be checking his surroundings for something. We couldn't tell who or even what his surroundings were. He was zoomed in on his face and the bush concealing him. "I just got permission to have a phone, but it only dials specific numbers. Believe me, I've tried to call you a thousand times."

"Permission to have a phone?" I repeated.

Val shushed me.

"I ended up stealing this from someone who is going to be looking for it very soon. The first thing you need to know is I'm safe. I'm not in danger here. Neither am I allowed to leave. This secret of the Sams and Sallys is so much bigger than we understood, Val. So much."

What does that mean? Stop talking in riddles!

"That night, I was taken by Sawyer and Aiden—assholes of the first fucking degree. Whatever bullshit they're spinning back home, I bet you saw through it, and you were right, baby. They're not murderers, but they're not who we believe either. Neither are they important."

"Not important?" Jaxson chimed in. "How are the guys who kid-napped him not important?"

"They can't tell you where I am. They don't know. Neither are they high enough in the food chain to find out. Aiden's just recruitment. The bosses handle their own business."

Recruitment? Bosses?

"Last week, a woman came to see us. She introduced herself as Kessler, and then we had a long chat about how much trouble you were causing. I don't know what she's going to do, but hearing her speech on protecting the program leads me to believe you two will be having a conversation sooner rather than later. That conversation will not be in the rattling back of a van."

Maverick stopped to peer around the hedges again. "I think I have a way out of here. A friend is going to cover for me, but it's a one-time thing. If it doesn't work... well, then you won't see this message. If it does, know that I love you, and I'm working to get back to you as fast as I can."

"Beaumont!"

A booming voice erupted from the speakers, blowing us all back.

"Goodbye."

"Wait! Maverick, no—!"

The screen went black.

Val stumbled to the couch, sitting down hard. I couldn't name the expression on her face, and it mirrored mine all the same. *What the fuck is going on?*

Ezra voiced the question for me. "Was that supposed to give us answers because all I have are more questions? Connelly is recruitment? A friend covered for him? What friend? And who shouted for him?"

All those questions were on my mind, but they weren't as loud as the most important thing Maverick said. "Maverick says he's safe, but he can't leave. The guy gets out to deliver this message, and then went right back to them. Why?"

"Because they'd know where to find him," Valentina rasped. "More than that, they know where to find us."

Well, we wanted a question answered. We got one.

Ezra broke the silence. "Kessler, isn't she—?"

"The CEO of Kessler Toys and head of the local chapter of Zeta Rho Sigma," Val finished. "I should've guessed she was up to her coral-pink eyeshadow in this."

Val got up to leave.

"Where are you going?" I asked.

She brandished my phone like a weapon. "Maverick said it. Kessler and I are due for a conversation."

"She's the CEO of a multimillion-dollar company," I said, tailing her out of the room. "We can't tie her to a chair in a sorority house and question her. She'll have her own team of private security, and if she knows about the *trouble* you've caused, she's not about to fall for a fake meeting to talk house business."

"Oh, she'll meet with me."

"In the middle of the night. The day before Christmas Eve."

That stopped her on the steps.

"She won't even pick up the phone."

"I can't just sit here, Ryder."

"You can't go charging off to her mansion to get shot climbing the gates either."

"The hell I can't."

I chased her down the stairs, scooped Val up in the front room, and tossed her screeching over my shoulder. I ignored the fists pounding my back.

"Maverick was smart," I said. "He got a message to us and made sure you saw it. We can't be stupid now." I climbed back up the stairs to Ezra and Jaxson. They easily helped me carry her to my bedroom.

Tossing Val on the mattress, I received a glare that peeled my head like a grape. She got a cocked brow in response.

"If we confront her without a plan to get Maverick back, she'll know he snitched," Jaxson said. "He could get punished for it and we won't be able to do a damn thing about it."

Groaning, Val flung herself on the pillows. "I know," she said. "I know you're right. But I just spent the last week thinking— You don't want to know what I was thinking. Now I see Maverick is trying to get back home to us. I can't let everything he's been through be for nothing."

"It won't be," I said. "I have an idea if you'll hear me out."

She hesitated, looking between us—likely adding up her chances of getting through us to the door.

"I'm listening."

THE MORNING, CHRISTMAS Eve rang in early.

"Mommy! Daddy, wake up!"

I cracked an eyelid, reading 7:14 a.m. on the clock. Very, very early.

"It's not Christmas yet, Little Moon," I said.

Adam found my hand under the covers and tried to tug me out. "It's Christmas Eve. I get to open one present on Christmas Eve."

"You can open two presents if you go down and check on breakfast for me," Val's side of the bed spoke up.

"Okay!" Adam took off running. *Checking on breakfast* always resulted in Chef letting him help with the cooking or setting up the table. Val just bought us an hour.

"All the parenting books say not to resort to bribery." I tossed an arm over her, burrowing my face in the back of her neck. "Those suckers don't know sleep deprivation."

She chuckled. "To be fair, we were the ones who stayed up till two in the morning."

"Worth it if we convinced you?"

"You did," she said softly. "We'll do things your way."

Pulling her closer, I searched under her hair for the sensitive spot beneath her ear. She hummed to my kisses.

"We can do a few other things my way."

"You can make anything into an innuendo, can't you?"

"Try me."

"Hmm. There's probably oatmeal on the menu this morning."

"I'll have that after I have you."

"I felt a weird lump under my arm the other day," she said.

"I can feel up all your lumps for you. Make sure everything's good in the name of health."

She swatted my backside. "I bet." Val moved between my legs. "Do I get to open my present early too?"

"Give me a minute to put a bow on it."

My phone went off.

"Ugh. It better not be work, or I'll chase you down the stairs and throw you back in bed."

"Yes, ma'am." A glance at the screen revealed it was Jacob. "I should get this. I forwarded Maverick's video to him last night. He said he'd get his guy on it right away."

"Answer it." Val put the phone to my ear herself.

"Hello?"

"Ryder." His deep voice flowed unhurried from the speaker. Even in an emergency, Jacob spoke calmly and authoritative. "Emmett is working on the video to see if he can pick up any background noise that'll point to his location. It's a long shot, but he won't give up until he's exhausted all options."

"Good."

"That's not the only reason I called. We spoke last week about acquiring the list of men that graduated Somerset in the same year as your mother."

I flicked to Valentina—who was closely studying my face. I closed the conversation down with Ezra and Jaxson. That didn't mean I was ignoring their concerns. Aiden Connelly stumbled on a secret my mother was willing to protect at all costs. We tortured him for over an hour. Who wouldn't ache for revenge?

"What do you got?"

"I can get you that list which will contain hundreds of names, but that is where my involvement ends."

"What?" I sat up. "Why?"

"I work for Caroline, Ryder. I cannot dig up my employer's past. Honestly, I'm contract-bound to report that you asked."

"No," I said. "Don't do that. You don't have to. I'm going to talk to Mom myself. I just... wanted to spare her this conversation for as long as possible." A thought occurred to me. "You know what I'm talking about, don't you?"

"I'm certain I don't."

I scoffed. "Of course you do. You don't keep my secrets, but you sure as hell keep Mom's."

"Good morning, Ryder. I hope you enjoy this day with your family."

Click.

"I'm firing his ass."

Val draped my arm around her shoulder. "No, you're not. You love him more than me."

"How much of that did you hear?"

"All of it." She kissed the peak of my chin. "Maybe it is time to go to Caroline directly. You don't have to stress about bringing me into it anymore. Aiden threatened you. He threatened her too. Caroline should know about it."

"She will." I flipped Val over and did away with the shorts and thong. "But maybe we should save the 'who's my daddy' game for after Christmas?"

"Fair enough."

I skimmed her soft lower lips, and Val wriggled away from me.

"Lock the door first." She kept rolling, hopping off the bed and darting to the piano. "You get to open a present today too."

"I was about to open my present."

She gave me a wry look while she popped my piano chair. A small brown package wrapped in twine appeared in her hand.

"You literally hid it right under my nose. Clever lady."

"Thank you. I thought so too."

Val hung over my shoulders, watching me tear off the paper. I pulled the hefty, triangular thing from the box. My smile was on my face before I saw it.

"A metronome."

"I noticed you didn't have one," she said. "It was the perfect gift for the man who has everything." She smooched my cheek. "That's why I didn't get you anything else."

"Wouldn't complain if you didn't. This is perfect." I snaked my arm around her waist. "Now, I believe I'm owed two presents."

"I don't remember agreeing to that."

"You will."

I lifted Val on the piano lid. She lay back, opening herself up to me completely. I ran my finger along her stomach, bringing her tank top up with me.

I've said it in all the ways and in every language I knew.

Val was the most gorgeous, sensual, intoxicating woman to ever walk this planet. Sometimes I looked at her and tried to understand how an accident of genes combined to make those swimmable eyes, soft curls, and bee-stung lips.

"You say I'm too beautiful to be legal, but damn, woman, have you seen yourself?"

She laughed. "You always get those heart-shaped googly eyes when my clothes are off. When they're on, I'm just as mortal as the rest of you."

"Wrong." I kissed the space between her breasts. "You are Aphrodite risen from the sea. Persephone, queen of life, hope, and spring. Athena, queen of—"

"—cracking open guys' heads and being smarter than everyone in the room."

"Exactly." I continued the journey down, nipping a path to her belly button where I stopped. Her breath caught as I kissed my way back up.

"Your present doesn't allow for teasing." Val tangled her fingers in my hair. "You're heading the wrong way, Shea."

I smacked her right cheek, getting a squeal out of her. "My present doesn't come with sass."

"Sass was part of the deal when you fell in love with me. Better buckle up. I'll be keeping you on your toes for the next seventy-odd years."

My tongue teased a circle around her nipple. "I'll be keeping you on your knees."

"Goodness. One after the other with these clit-swelling innuendos. They're your superpower, baby."

No, this is my superpower.

Draping her legs over my shoulders, I dropped between them, cock straining at the sweet, musky scent beckoning me home. I swiped between her folds, collecting her juices on my tongue.

Val let out a long, drawn-out hiss similar to a teakettle preparing to scream. And she would.

I plundered her to my heart's content—dipping in and out of her well, then coming up for air to steal hers, sucking her swollen clit.

"Yes, Ryder. Uh, that feels so good." She fisted my hair hard enough to pull it out. "Feel free to open this gift every morning."

I stole one more taste, and drew back. Valentina vibrated with need. She hooked her legs around me to make sure I didn't go anywhere.

Like I could. I'm staining thousand-dollar pajama bottoms with pre-cum.

Maverick was spot on calling Valentina an addiction. My hands were shaking on the metronome in ache of my next fix.

"Metronomes measure tempo. Not too fast and not too slow." A gentle *tick, tick, tick* filled the air. "When you're lost in a piece."

My pants pooled around my ankles.

"The music consumes you and shuts you in a world where nothing else exists."

I splayed my fingers on her thighs, opening her to me.

"It's easy to get excited and lose your pace." I sunk inside to the hilt, catching my breath on a groan. "We won't have that problem anymore."

Tick.

In.

Tick.

Out.

Tick.

In.

I pumped a slow, steady pace—undoing us both. Val's sweet pussy swallowed me to the hilt, and kissed my tip on the way out.

"Faster," she cried.

"Can't."

"Ryder, your life is at stake here!"

I laughed—light, rich, and full like it'd become since Val upended my life. It was hard to imagine there was ever a time I wanted to live without her. People said teenage boys were fatally stupid. They were one hundred percent accurate about me.

"Don't come until I say. The piece isn't over."

She whimpered, arching her back on the piano. I held her up and angled deeper, hitting that spot to the tick-ticking. Val's fevered cries rose in pitch.

My balls tightened. Muscles constricted. Sweat beaded on my brow. It was me who wouldn't make it to the end.

Valentina was a masterpiece in and of herself. Silky waves fanned on dark maple. The contrast of her pale, perfect skin mimicked ivory breasts topped with jasper jewels. Right then, I wished my talent was painting to capture the perfect image that was her. Or photography.

The pressure built till there was only one way to let it out.

I exploded inside of her, crashing and dying on a rocky bed of triumph when she came so hard she slid off the piano and we fell over the bench.

"Ow," I said. "Never been injured mid-ejaculation before."

Val covered me in kisses. She was hanging on to me like my own personal koala bear and didn't seem interested in letting me go. "Don't you love that we still have firsts?"

Bang! Bang! Bang!

"Mom! Dad! It's time to open presents."

Val sighed. "Once again, my master calls."

Chapter Seven

Valentina

It was a wonderful Christmas. Shadowed by Maverick's absence. Lightened by the knowledge wherever he was, Maverick wasn't harmed. They were strange feelings to hold at the same time. But I was a pro at loving four different men in equally different ways. I could both miss him and be relieved he was safe at the same time. I could also be pissed as shit.

I stood in the parking lot of Kessler Toys, balling and unballing my fists.

Maverick said Aiden was a cog in the machine. The deliveryman.

I couldn't say where Kessler fit into this equation. All I knew is she was the person I was meant to question. She held on to Maverick's location.

Taking a deep breath, I let it out slowly. *I know what to do. We've gone over it a dozen times. She will tell me where Maverick is.*

I repeated the mantra to myself as I locked the car and shoved the keys in my bag. My cell went off. I fished my phone out and hitched it back up my shoulder.

"Oh, miss." A woman in the car beside me rolled down her window. "You dropped something."

Sure enough my key fob for the manor's main gate lay on the concrete.

"Thank you so much," I said, turning back to pick it up. "Have a nice day."

"You too." Starting the car, she rolled her window up.

I got out of her way and paused in front of my trunk to read Jaxson's text.

Jaxson: You okay? Sure you don't want us there?

Me: Of course I want you here, but

Screech!

The world rocked, throwing me off my feet. I hit the pavement hard.

What? What happened?

The fall dazed me. Vision spinning, moments passed before I realized someone was shouting. A horn blew.

I blinked and my fallen phone came into focus. The second sight to meet my eyes was the melded back ends of my and the woman's car. She crashed into me, and I was thrown.

Crashed into me? How—?

"—wrong with you?!" The sound returned with a pop. "How fast were you going? Did you see me backing up?"

Pink heels ran out from beneath the car, and from my position on the ground, I saw a pair of blue sneakers hit the pavement and start running.

"Hey! Hey, come back here!"

"Ma'am, are you alright?" I came to as a pair of strong hands lifted me under the arms. "Did you see that? It was horrible. Some fool came racing through the parking lot and slammed into that woman."

More people rushed to help us. I thanked them, checking myself over, and ensuring I was okay as I said I was. I had a scrape on my wrist that was starting to bleed. Other than that, I was fine.

"The jerk just ran off." The woman was still raging. "Who does something like that?"

"Why don't you come in and sit down?" someone asked. "You can call the police inside."

Breaking free, I checked the damage. The collision was enough to knock all one hundred and ten pounds of me to the ground, but it didn't do much to Ryder's Bentley other than scratch the paint job.

"I'm fine." I checked my phone for the time. "I have to get going. Hope you catch up to the person who did this."

"Oh, I'll catch up to them."

The lady stomped around to the license plate. I didn't stay to see more than that. It was just a little scrape and some dirt on my clothes. It wouldn't stop me from getting to this meeting. A meeting that was surprisingly easy to arrange. So easy, I suspected she knew my wanting to talk to her about another charity fundraiser was bullcrap.

"Whatever gets me through the door," I said to my reflection in the bathroom. Quickly I cleaned myself up, dabbing away the blood. That done, I asked for a bandage from the receptionist, then stepped inside the elevator.

It carried me ten stories and dinged open on the floor Kessler had to herself. The perks of being the boss.

"Good morning." A petite young woman rose from behind the desk. "You must be Miss Moon."

We shook hands.

"Are you all right?" she asked, noticing the bandage.

"I'm fine, thank you."

"Please, sit, and I'll call you when she's ready."

Nice power move. Making sure I know who is in charge. If only you knew too, Kessler.

I sat without complaint and fussed with my phone. We were two days into the new year. That was the earliest Kessler's secretary was willing to schedule me after I finally got ahold of her.

Another holiday we had to celebrate without Maverick.

I flipped through the photos of us popping streamers and kiss-attacking Adam at nine o'clock on New Year's Eve. He was seven. No way he was staying up until midnight.

My gaze drifted to the plaque bearing her name. Did she take another trip up to see Maverick after that video was made? Did they have another chat? Did she think about him and what we were going through even once while she was sipping wine and opening presents with her family?

My phone cracked in my grip. Attempts to stay calm were not working.

"Miss Moon?" Her secretary pushed open the door for me. "Mrs. Kessler is ready for you."

Ophelia Kessler did not rise from her desk when I came in. The only thing that moved was the corner of her lips, turning up with my boiling temper.

Don't fucking smirk at me.

"Hello, Valentina. Lovely to see you again."

I sat in the chair before her desk, eyes trained on her like the coiled viper would strike at any moment.

"Did you have a nice holiday?"

"That's kind of an insensitive question. How nice could my holiday be when my boyfriend is missing?"

"Oh, of course." She rested a hand on her chest. "I heard about that. I'm so sorry, Valentina. I can't imagine what you're going through."

"I'm really glad to hear that you're sorry. You can make it up to me by taking me to Maverick."

A pregnant pause smothered the room. I used to think that was a strange phrase—pregnant pause. Now I understood why no other could fit.

Slightly widening eyes. Stiffening chin. Leaning back in her chair to create distance. And me, baring my teeth. Fighting another urge to explode. Bursting with the pain and anger I felt for months.

A lot went on in this pause. It was loaded with meaning, and charged to blow.

"What do you mean?" she asked, voice light. "I can't take you to him. I don't know where he is."

"Mrs. Kessler, this will go a lot faster if you don't lie to me. Matter of fact, let's make that a rule," I said. "Lie to me once, and the whole world finds out about the program."

"Program?"

"Feigning ignorance counts as lying."

"I'm afraid you're going to have to help me out here, Valentina. I'd love to have a discussion with you once I know the topic of conversation."

I said nothing. Simply pulled up the video on my phone, and hit play.

"Man, I wish I could say this to you face-to-face. I wish I could see your face. Touch you. Hold you—"

"Oops. That part is just for me." I skipped ahead. "This is the part you should listen to."

"Last week, a woman came to see us. She introduced herself as Kessler, and then we had a long chat about how much trouble you were causing. I don't know what she's going to do, but hearing her speech on protecting the program—"

Kessler vaulted out of her seat. "Shut that off."

"—to believe you two will be having a conversation sooner rather than later."

"Shut it off now!"

I pressed pause. "I'm here for that conversation. Do you remember the topic now?"

"You will delete that video this instant—"

"You're not making the rules here, Mrs. Kessler. I am. Sit down."

She didn't move.

"Sit!"

Stiffly, forcing unresponsive limbs to work, Kessler claimed her seat.

"I've had about e-fucking-nough with these games, lies, and half-truths. The next thing out of your mouth will be Maverick's location, or this video goes viral in an hour."

"You do not understand what you're doing."

I shrugged. "That's what everyone keeps telling me, but you know what, I'm going to do it anyway. If no one can bother to tell me the truth, I can't be bothered to sit quietly like a good little president. I will release this video in the next"—I flicked to the clock—"two minutes if you don't come clean."

Kessler folded her hands on the desk. She was making an effort to appear relaxed and in control. I saw through to the clenched teeth and swirling anger in her eyes.

"Heaven knows what you hoped to accomplish here, but I assure you it will not work. If you release that video to the media, you will not make it out of this building."

"Is that a threat?"

"That's a guarantee."

I cracked a smile. "If I don't walk out of here in twenty minutes, my boyfriends will release the video in my place. So kill me, Kessler. You can explain why your men hauled my body out the service entrance while the cops are questioning your little kidnapping scheme."

"Kill you?" She laughed. "You truly think you're in some kind of action movie. We're all one-dimensional villains and you're the tough heroine weathering the fight till the end. No one is going to kill you, Valentina. If you release that video, I will have you arrested."

"That's a risk I'm willing to take. Are you?" I held her gaze without flinching.

"One minute."

RYDER

Mom set up in the backyard with a canvas, easel, and soft music. She said she reached that age where she got to fill her days with activities, lunch dates, and reading by the pool. She was embracing it wholeheartedly.

I stopped short of the porch, looking down at the list of men who graduated Somerset the same year as my mother. I printed it off that morning but had yet to do anything with it other than fold and stuff it in my pocket.

The next step involved hours of looking up people, tracking down photos, cross-referencing common names with the man I was looking for. It was hours and hours of work, and all I'd have to lie to her about unless she shortened my search and told me now.

"Mom."

"Yes, darling." She dabbed clouds in the corner of the canvas.

"I need to speak to you about something."

"Come sit with me."

The only place to sit was on the blanket beneath her stool. I sat down, draping my arms over my knees, and looking over the expanse of green. Phantom children ran across the lawn—laughing and playing like this was a happy place that could hold good memories. Since Valentina, Adam, Jaxson, Ezra, and Maverick moved in, it became that place.

"Mom, something happened that we need to talk about."

"Sounds serious." She pushed my hair back from my eyes, smearing paint on my forehead. "What's wrong?"

"You know what's been happening with Valentina, Maverick, and the fraternity," I began. "Val had another *argument* with Aiden Connelly. He threatened to come after us if she didn't drop it."

"I'd like to see him try."

"There are ways to hurt someone without laying a hand on them," I said evenly. "Aiden Connelly said he will go wide with the news I'm not Benjamin Shea's son."

Mom's hand jerked on the canvas—slashing a black line on the old-fashioned cabin. "Excuse me?"

"It's obvious, apparently," I went on. "Something about widow's peaks and rare eye colors. He's shocked no one noticed it before."

"Ryder," she cried. "How could—? That's not—!"

"Don't," I cut in. "Please, don't lie. Honestly, I think I've always known. When I was younger, kids used to ask me if I was adopted because my mom was pretty, but my dad was ugly. That's the kind of plain talk you get when you're seven. Ever since I would study Benjamin and wonder why we weren't alike. Connelly confirmed what I knew deep down. That man is not my blood."

Mom clamped my shoulder. "Yes, he is. How could you believe that lying blackmailer? Benjamin is your father, and if he dares to say otherwise, I will bury him in so much litigation, he won't see the sun for years." She shoved off the stool. "Where is Jacob?"

I ran after her. "Mom."

"Of all the vicious, sick rumors—"

"Mom, stop!"

"I will take care of this, Ryder. Think no more about it."

"I am not related to that violent, abusive, cheating piece of shit! Why did you let me believe I am?!"

"Because!" She whirled on me, pulling me up short. "If you're not, we will be evicted from this house without the clothes on our backs. You will be fired from the company. Your inheritance given to distant relations we've never met. The contract formed to put your grandparents' restaurant in every mall Shea Industries builds—dissolved. The legacy they left for you, your aunts, uncles, and cousins—wiped away.

"But you know what will remain in the ashes of our broken lives, my son?" Harsh lines around her eyes and mouth turned my mother into a different person. "A strong motive for wanting Benjamin Shea to disappear."

She grasped my chin, drilling deep into my eyes. "You are his son. I would die to protect the fact."

Mom cracked the sliding glass storming into the house. I heard her calling for Jacob from outside.

Looking down, I removed the list from my pocket.

I expected her reasons for lying to me were strong ones. Stronger than shame and relying on her need to protect her child. I was ready to blow those reasons up with the reminder I wasn't a child. I'd been ready to combat every argument, but it was my speech she blew up.

It's not just our lives that would crumble if the truth came out. I could survive the loss of the house and the company, but my family couldn't. And a reopening of the investigation into Benjamin Shea's disappearance...

The papers crinkled in my fist.

I should throw these away. Burn them on the fire pit and let sleeping secrets lie.

I've done just fine in my life without knowing my biological father. I wasn't some simpering child crying for my daddy. I became a man without him. I'd live my life with my beautiful family without him.

Besides, there was no guarantee he was one of the names on this list. Mom could've conceived me in a random, drunken hookup to take her mind off being married to the devil.

Let this go, a voice whispered. *A stranger isn't worth the implosion of your life.*

Throw the list away.

Folding it up, I stuffed it back in my pocket and went inside.

It would take hours, days, weeks to get through everyone.

I'd better get started.

VALENTINA

"One minute," I repeated. "What's it going to be?"

Kessler picked up the phone. "Hello? Yes, this is she. Please have the authorities on standby. No, I don't need security up here yet. Hopefully it won't have to come to that."

I blinked lazily as she returned it to its cradle. "Is that supposed to scare me? Haven't I made it clear I'll happily go to jail? My lawyers will have me out in twenty minutes."

"That entirely depends on their ability to locate you."

"Ahh." I leaned back in my seat. "Now we're getting somewhere. Just in time.

"Eleven.

"Ten.

"Nine."

Kessler leaped from her seat as I hit the share button. "That's enough."

"Seven.

"Six," I continued. "Here's hoping my black van takes me to Maverick. Three. Two."

"You've made your point, Valentina."

"One."

I hit share.

"All right," she burst out. "I will answer your questions. Delete it. Now."

"I'll delete it in front of you *after* we talk."

Her lips twisted. "Fine." Kessler stuck her head out. "Emily, take your break."

I tracked her locking the door, lowering the blinds, and then taking her phone off the hook. Each act bound me tighter with apprehension. This is what you did before you strangle someone with a phone cord, not spilled a long-held secret.

"What is—?"

"Be quiet," she snapped. Kessler pulled a document out of her desk. "Read it. Sign it."

I stared at the piece of paper, and *Contract of Nondisclosure* written in big block letters across the top.

"I know what you're thinking. This single flimsy piece of paper can't mean much. I'll sign, and then the old woman will tell me what I need to know," she said. "We will have a discussion after this paper is signed, but if the details of that discussion are made public or shared with anyone outside this room, you will receive ten years in prison and be slapped with a fine that'll bankrupt your great-grandchildren. And believe me, your lawyers are not better than mine. Do we understand each other?"

I looked from her to the paper. "Perfectly."

I read it carefully, confirmed her threats were not empty, and signed.

"There," I announced, sliding it back to her. "Tell me where Maverick is. What is the program and why is he in it?"

"Don't be ridiculous. It's the middle of the workday, and I have a call with the head of the London branch in twenty minutes."

Rage flared hot and wild. "What? You said you'd tell me if I signed. Was this some trick to bind me in the contract? Because if you think that's going to stop me—"

"No. It's not a trick precisely because I know it won't stop you." She eyed me in the middle of pulling a card and pen from her drawer. "I wouldn't stop if it was Gerald."

I wasn't certain who Gerald was. I assumed he was the man smiling and holding her in the pictures on her desk.

"It's no use telling you where your boyfriend is. You wouldn't make it past the gate," she said. "Be at this location tomorrow morning at nine. Come alone. Nonnegotiable. Bring that cellphone and the video. Also nonnegotiable." She dropped the card on my palm. "Now leave."

"No."

She cocked a brow. "Excuse me?"

"No," I repeated. "I'm not leaving until you give me a reason to trust you. Show up to some shady location in the middle of the night so I can be the next one to disappear for months? You must think I'm an idiot."

Kessler studied me for a long time. Long enough it became uncomfortable.

"Since the founding of the Zeta Rho Sigma house, we've been running a secret government program that exclusively recruits Sallys and Sams. Candidates do not know their admittance into the house is an interview for those coveted spots. They are also not aware they're chosen until they are brought to the farm for training. You are currently undergoing the interview process, Valentina Moon." She stood up. "Between you and me, it's not going well."

My jaw worked. *Secret government program? Recruits Sams and Sallys?*

"There you are. I shared the most important part of the puzzle. Your need to hear the rest will see you at that address tomorrow. We will have a nice long drive to discuss your future in Zeta Rho."

Slowly, my feet carried me to the door. I couldn't speak. I couldn't turn back. I couldn't understand how I was going forward.

I found myself standing in front of the elevator, waiting for it to carry me away, and a single certainty overcame me.

I didn't understand anything that was going on.

Not a single damn thing.

THE NEXT MORNING, I settled Adam in the living room with his puppy, breakfast, and favorite movie. Jaxson conked out on the couch beside him. He stayed late at work the night before to watch a recording session.

I popped a kiss on Adam's forehead. "Put Daddy to bed on time, love."

He giggled. "I will."

"I'll be back later. Call Cara if you need anything."

Adam bobbed his head, already absorbed in the movie.

Now was my chance. Ryder was working in his office. Ezra was visiting his mother. Jaxson was currently asleep, and Caroline was enjoying a book in the living room across the hall. A text to all of them saying I was going out and would be back later would do the trick, so that's what I did.

I backed Ryder's second car down the driveway. The GPS chirped directions to a house twenty-five minutes from me. I looked up the place online. It wasn't Kessler's home unless she was the kind of millionaire who preferred two-bedroom bungalows to mansions.

I drove to the house and parked on the curb. Kessler told me nine o'clock. I was here at eight forty-five.

Hopefully she believes early is on time too.

I looked up and down the normal, everyday neighborhood. Sturdy oak trees lined both sides of the street. Two houses down, a couple of kids scrambled up one, screeching and swinging off the branches.

This isn't the best place to throw me in the back of a van and carry me to my final resting place. But then, why bother with the shadowy location when I already agreed to get in the van willingly?

Despite Kessler revealing one of the cards in her hand, this was feeling more and more like a giant mistake.

I climbed out of the car and headed up the drive. A noise behind turned me around.

A small blue car lumbered down the lane. I couldn't make out much through the tinted windows, and I was staring hard. Strange as it was, I sensed the person inside staring back at me.

Is that Kessler?

The car slowed nearing the house, and stopped. I approached them. My hand reached for the handle as the doors unlocked.

"Moon."

Snapping up, I spun at the familiar voice.

Aiden Connelly stood on the front porch—raging mad.

"You were told to come alone. You can't obey orders once in your fucking life, can you?"

My shock at seeing him was swallowed by indignation. "I did come alone. I don't—"

The driver hit the gas. They sped off down the street with a blast of wind that blew my peplum top up.

"—know who that is," I finished. "Thought it was Kessler, who I'm supposed to be meeting instead of you." I stormed up to him. "Where is she?"

Aiden smirked that smirk. It was everything in me to not punch his teeth in.

"Simmer down. She's here. Mrs. Kessler decided in her infinite wisdom to hold this meetup at my place—thanks for that, by the way."

"You're welcome."

The smirk curled around the edges. "You're finally going to be let in on the big secret, and when you are, I'll expect an apology in the form of a huge check for emotional damages. All three of your wealthy boyfriends can chip in." He flicked over my shoulder. "I'd quite like that car too."

"My car?"

"Yes, I'll definitely take the car."

"Settle your differences on your own time." Kessler's voice was soon followed by the woman herself stepping out of the house. "Valentina."

"Ophelia."

I might have imagined the quick quirk of her lips. It was gone too fast for me to be sure.

"Did you bring your phone?"

"Yes."

"Open it. Pull up the video," she ordered.

I did so. Kessler plucked it from my hands and passed it to Aiden.

"Know what to do?"

"Of course, ma'am. Delete every trace of the video, then send a message from her phone to Shea, Van Zandt, and Lennox. When they open it, a massive virus will download and wipe out their systems."

"Hey!" I made a swipe for my phone. Aiden dodged.

"Just in case you're lying and they all have copies of the video."

"I'm not," I gritted. "Don't do it, Aiden. Ezra is working on a project worth a quarter of his grade."

"Pleading mercy for the man who tortured me? You must be joking. I hope he doesn't back up his files."

Kessler threw her arm out in front of me, stopping me from chasing after him. "I thought you understood the stakes by now, but apparently it still hasn't sunk in. This must be done, Valentina. Our secrecy is our best defense."

I let it go only because Ezra did back up his files. Adam accidentally spilled chocolate milk on his laptop in the middle of writing a term paper. That on top of living with Maverick for years had us well versed in virus protection and recovery.

"Who is our?" I asked.

"We'll continue this in the car. I parked a street over."

I let her lead me away. An understated black Ford beeped to life under Kessler's command. I hesitated reaching for the handle.

If there's even a chance this isn't one big joke and she's taking you to Maverick, you have to get in the car.

That was all the pep talk I needed.

"Where are we going?"

"It's not far."

I leveled a hard look on her. "Our conversation isn't going to consist of more vague answers, is it?"

"I apologize. It's a hazard of the job. You get used to answering questions without actually answering them." She put the car in gear. "I apologize for this too."

"For wha—?"

Hands seized me from behind. I screamed—a helpless noise quickly muffled by a damp cloth slapped over my mouth. Sweet, sickly fumes fogged my mind.

"Relax, Valentina." Kessler blurred around the edges. "We'll be there soon."

RYDER

"I should be passed out right now."

"My family drama is more interesting than whatever was playing on your eyelids."

"I was dreaming about a very naked Valentina and a bottle of honey."

"Then, I sincerely apologize."

Jaxson snorted. "Are you sure about this, man? What if this guy was a year older or younger than her? We could spend hours looking these guys up for nothing."

"I've been through the what-ifs a thousand times. Jacob won't help me from this point on, and I can't take information like this outside the family. One shady private investigator and all my mom's fears come true."

"All right." Jaxson set his laptop across from mine and picked up the two top sheets from my stack. "I'll do half. You do half. We'll knock this shit out."

I observed him. "That's it? You're not going to ask me why I'm doing this, or why I won't let it go?"

"You're Ryder Shea. You never let things go."

"I'm serious."

Jaxson's expression shone with rare sincerity. Not because he wasn't a guy to take things seriously, but because he never let people see it when he did.

"I can't say what's the right thing to do," Jaxson said. "All I know is if my mom wasn't gone and was actually out there somewhere waiting for me to find her, I wouldn't give up until I did."

I nodded. "Slightly different situation since your mom would know if she had a kid, and would've chosen to leave your ass."

"Fuck off. You know what I'm saying."

Cracking a grin, I said, "I do. Thanks, man."

"We gonna do this, or hug and kiss through the tears?"

He's back.

Adam was getting under my mom's feet. Ezra had his own project to take care of. Valentina was off on a drive. There was nothing to stop me. No more excuses.

"Let's do it."

In silence we worked, looking up each name, tracking down their social media, struggling to confirm the faces on the screen linked up with the typed names on the pages. Adam wandered in at one point and wiggled his way on Jaxson's lap. Jaxson played music on his laptop for him, and Adam seemed content to stay there.

"How much have you gotten through?" he asked over "Hey You" by Pink Floyd.

"Seventeen."

"I've ruled out thirty-one."

"What?" I pushed out of my seat. "How?"

"You get good at this stuff when your job is tracking down obscure bands the sound tech heard that one time in a bar he can't remember. Somerset University is a prestigious school. So far, they've all made where they graduated bold and clear on pages."

"I've been looking at that too, but it still took me twenty minutes to sort through the fifty John Kellys that showed up."

"I narrowed it down by friend list. Caroline probably didn't fall for an awkward loner who spent his weekends hiding out in the dorm and growing mushrooms under the bed. The guy would have friends. Those friends would link up with him on social media. Each name I check off, I search through their friends for more."

"Genius," I muttered. "Why didn't I think of that?"

"We can't assume he looks like you, but I'm betting you got at least one of the features you didn't get from Caroline, from him. White, male, and dark hair is what I'm going with. That excludes a lot of guys straight off the top. Once we have the list of men he could be, where do we go from there?"

"Direct approach. Call them up and ask if they remember a Caroline from college. Say she's getting in contact with old friends. All I need is one to say they used to date, and I've got him."

"When's Mommy coming home?" Adam asked. The whole conversation was going over his head and he wasn't that interested anyway.

"Not sure," Jaxson asked. "I'll call her. Shea, use the friends list. If we're lucky, we'll get through all these by tomorrow."

I tackled the list with renewed vigor. My mom would kill me if she found out and this was probably a waste of time, but for years I could do nothing about the secret Valentina dropped in my lap. At least now I was doing something.

"Voicemail," Jaxson said after Val didn't pick up the second call. "She'll call us back when she gets our messages."

"Can we make a special lunch for her?" Adam asked.

"Quesadillas?"

"Yes!"

"All right. Give me twenty minutes... and then... we'll..." Jaxson trailed off.

I raised my head. Jaxson was staring wide-eyed at his screen. "What's up?"

"Ryder," he breathed. "You need to see this."

Adam pointed. "Look. It's your daddy."

The sentence punched a hole through me once, then again when Jaxson did not correct him. Jerkily, I circled the desk to what had them both fixated. My mouth opened but nothing came out.

It was me.

In twenty years with wings of gray at my temples and lines around my eyes, but all the same, it was me. Full, thick raven hair blew wild in the picture, pointing to the windy day. A good day if the wide smile that pronounced his cleft jaw was anything to go by. Under his arm was a pretty, petite woman who looked up at him with adoring eyes. But Charles Nelson looked at me... with silver eyes.

"It has to be him." Jaxson's voice reached me from far away. "Ryder Charles Shea. Your mom gave you his name."

As he said it, I knew it had to be true. It had to be him.

"You're practically his clone," Jaxson said.

I moved through sludge, staggering to my laptop to type him in, read everything, know everything.

"Now we know why she let him go."

That dragged me out of my fog. "What? What do you mean?"

"I mean when you popped out the spitting image of him, your mom couldn't afford for anyone to see you both together and figure it out. It's likely why she didn't tell you. If you showed up on this guy's doorstep, he'd know you were his, and if he fought for a place in your life, you'd lose everything."

"Are you trying to tell me something?"

"I'm saying, think carefully what you do next. Because this is him, Ryder. He has to be."

A beep sounded, alerting us to a notification.

"It's Val," Jaxson said. "Told you she'd get us right back." Jaxson tickled Adam into submission.

The same email notification came up on my screen. I left it for Jaxson to open while I typed in Charles Nelson. I hovered over the first name in the search, and clicked.

The screen went black.

"What the?" I jabbed the power button. "What happened? Am I plugged in?"

"I am and mine just went dead... after I opened the message from Val."

My brows furrowed. "Where did she say she was going today?"

Chapter Eight

Valentina

I shifted on a soft surface. Remains of a dream drifted through my mind, confusing me.

I was with Ryder, Ezra, and Jaxson. They were floating by my side in the pool, cheering me on with tips as something, or someone, floated beneath—waiting for me to sink.

"Don't panic, Val. Trying to save your life is how you lose it."

"Let go. The water will carry you."

Let go.

My eyelids fluttered. Was I home? Was I hearing Jaxson and Ezra? Is that why they were in my dream?

"Valentina... up."

There was a voice.

"Wake up."

Peeling my eyes open, the world came into focus on a single face.

"Ah. Finally, we can get started."

"What... happened?"

"Forgive me. The exact location of the farm is information you're not cleared to know."

It started coming back to me. A thump from the back seat. Then a cloth over my mouth.

"Ever hear of a blindfold?"

Gingerly, I pushed myself up, scanning my new surroundings.

I looked to be in a cabin or bunkhouse. Opposite of the summer camp cabins I'd see in movies and wish I could go to growing up. The twelve beds, including the one I was lying on, were draped with soft, downy comforters and made neatly.

Each bunk had a bedside table covered with various things from the person who claimed it. Books, glasses case, flowers, and journals. The whole place was clean, charming, and smelled faintly of mint.

"I get distracted for a second, you peek under the blindfold, and it's all for naught," Kessler said. "The chloroform removes any doubt."

I scoffed. "Believe it or not, I don't even care. Maverick's here. Take me to him."

"Maverick is completing an assignment at the moment and cannot be interrupted. You will see him after he's done." She raised her voice on the last sentence, covering my protests.

"I figured you'd like to use this opportunity to talk." She held out her hands. "We can speak freely here. Go ahead. Ask your questions."

I hesitated. Part of me didn't believe she was serious. After everything we've been through over the years, it turned out all it took was to get on Kessler's nerves and she'd bring me up here for a girl chat.

This is my chance to know the truth. And I will get it.

"Why?" I asked. "Why did you take him?"

Kessler's expression remained neutral. "The decision to invite Mr. Beaumont into the program wasn't made by me. Aiden made the case he was the ideal candidate, and I said no for the simple fact he wasn't a Sam. I was overruled."

"You were?"

"We all answer to someone."

I accepted that. Kessler said this was a government program. Naturally people were above her.

"Ideal candidate for what? What is the program?"

Kessler got to her feet. "Walk with me."

"No, thank you. The last time I went on a stroll with you, it ended with a long nap. We're alone in here and I'm closest to the exit. I'm staying until you stop delaying and answer my questions."

"Fair enough." She reclaimed her spot on the opposite bench. "I shouldn't have to ask this because you're president, but I will anyway. Do you know the story of the first Sally?"

"Yes. She gave her life to stop a school shooting."

"She did," Kessler replied. "Sally was a brave young woman, and in her honor, the sorority and fraternity were formed. What many don't know is the story did not end there. Sally's mother approved the request for her daughter's name to be in connection with Zeta Rho and Nu Alpha, as long as it stood for the same principles her daughter died for. She would not have her child's legacy be beer pong and hazing."

"Understandable."

"Under her direction, the Sams and Sallys became something else entirely, and as a member of the clandestine services, she saw potential."

I looked around. "Sally's mother founded the program. To do what exactly?"

"To do exactly what you're thinking, Valentina. We train them to serve their country."

"For the CIA? NSA?"

"Not exactly," she said, inclining her head. "Their work may make it through those channels, but our Sallys and Sams do not report to either agency. I want you to imagine a wind-up toy. It's running out of steam—slowing to a halt. What we do is pick it up, wind it, and send it racing down its path.

"A young man like Maverick Beaumont has no incentive to join the CIA," she said. "A sense of duty is all well and good, but for a person in his position, he knows he can do his part by taking over his father's company and creating technology the government can use to protect the country. Some would say that's the most valuable contribution he could make."

"It is," I said. "Maverick Tech has tons of government contracts. I see how hard they work to contribute to our defense. What more do you want from him?"

"People will always want more from those like him, because he's the kind of person who can achieve more." Kessler laid a hand over mine. "Maverick's path is set. As much as the NSA, NASA, or other organizations want to recruit him, he has no compelling reason to say yes."

"So, that's what this program is about. Making sure the Mavericks of this world don't have a choice."

She tossed her head. "No, that's— Forgive me, I'm not explaining this properly. Let's go back to the wind-up toy. We don't take the toy, lock it up, or knock it off course. We give it the ability to continue on its path with new strength and purpose. Instead of losing bright, talented, young minds to the private sector, we forge alliances. Maverick will continue on to do what he was meant to do, but as an agent of the program. The difference between working with his government, and viewing his government as a business opportunity."

The picture began forming in my mind. "They're spies," I said bluntly. "Spies that don't go out into the field, or go on action movie adventures, but spies that work for the government all the same. Like you said, they're the bright young minds who dedicate their talents to medicine, science, or technology, instead of a job where they must hide from everyone they love." I stood, pacing the room. "I understand the logic. What I don't understand is why you go about it the way you do? Kidnapping people off the street and gaslighting everyone in their life is psychotic."

"A harsh, but fair way to put it. Our methods are extreme, but secrecy is our best defense. Naturally if it got out Zeta Rho, Nu Alpha, and the rest were recruiting grounds for a government program, exactly how many pledges do you think we'd get a year? Not to mention the danger you'd all be in by our enemies.

"The brothers and sisters must be assessed without their knowledge, and when a candidate is chosen, they are brought here, told exactly what I am telling you, and then given the choice to accept or reject. Those that accept are given cover stories to explain their absence back home. Those that reject are relocated to different schools and bound under so many contracts, agreements, and threats, if they sneeze a word of this, they'll be jailed. Our rejection rate is almost zero."

"Course it fucking is," I cried.

"Because," she continued, "we're careful in our screening. We choose those we're certain will accept. And that should tell you something, Valentina. Maverick is still here. He chose this. You may not trust me, but I assume you trust him. Would he still be here if what we were doing was evil or nefarious?"

I narrowed on her. "That's excellent emotional manipulation. Maverick is here because he *can't leave*. He had to escape to get a message to me."

"Certainly he did. Once he agreed to join the program, he wasn't allowed contact with you, family, or friends until training is complete. None of the recruits are fond of that rule. In Mr. Beaumont's case, he had the smarts to get around it. Further proof he's perfect for the program. Aiden was right to recommend him."

"You're doing a great job dressing it up like it's all harmless. Just a bunch of people doing their duty for queen and country. But if you're in the mood for answering questions, tell me, was Leighton in the program?"

Something flickered in Kessler's eyes—too quick for me to place. "She was. The majority of presidents are in the program. It's necessary. They're perfectly placed to choose the best candidates."

"Do the majority of presidents murder students and call you to clean up the bodies? You were the friends Leighton spoke of that night. Don't lie and say you weren't."

Kessler remained blank. "I have no intention of lying to you. While I did not receive the call myself, Leighton did phone the woman she reports to after the murder of Logan Bilius."

I jerked, rocking back. I asked for the truth and still hearing his name said so casually threw me. "You do know about Logan," I rasped.

"I know quite a lot of things about... quite a lot of things."

"She killed him and your people covered it up. How many times have you performed that service?" I demanded.

"Okay, hold on." Kessler stood to face me. "Obviously, there are times when difficult decisions must be made for the good of the whole. It is not our practice that those decisions are carried out by those in the program. Kill orders are best left to those trained and licensed to kill. Not twenty-one-year-old sorority presidents."

"Then why—"

"Leighton, Reagan, and her friends had a fundamental misunderstanding of what they were chosen to do. It happens," she said. "The duty to serve becomes ingrained, and they feel they must right every wrong they see—especially when they have the training and knowledge to do something about it.

"After planning to rape Sofia Richards and attempting to rape you—"

Again I staggered back. She truly knew everything.

"—Leighton decided a dangerous, soulless man like that could not run free to target other women. She killed him by her own choice, and after explaining her reasons, it was decided not to let her waste in prison over the likes of Logan Bilius. As I said, choices are made for the greater good. Would you have wanted her convicted for what she did?"

I was surprised to find myself shaking my head. "I didn't shed a tear then, and I don't shed them now for Logan. It was more the knowledge the woman could literally get away with murder that freaked me out. How was I supposed to know if I was next? Or if that's what really happened to Maverick?"

"Believe me, we made it clear Leighton was never to do anything like that again. In the future, she was to report it, not take matters into her own hands. She argued. The situation became heated, and Leighton was removed from the program along with Reagan and Priscilla."

"You fired her?"

"Yes," Kessler replied. "I told you how it works. Since she was no longer in the program, she couldn't be president or continue going to Somerset University. Leighton died in a crash before the transfer went through. Reagan and Priscilla were transferred."

I stopped listening after died in the crash. "Leighton really is dead? The crash wasn't faked."

"We received a copy of the autopsy report. The body in the car was Leighton."

I sat down hard. "But I thought... I could've sworn it was her."

"Who, dear?"

"Never mind," I said, shaking my head. "It's not important. Why did Leighton want me for this program? Because she did, didn't she? I always felt she was too interested in me."

"She was. You were Leighton's top pick before things went wrong, and we began questioning her judgment. With her no longer in the picture, I see for myself that you exhibit the qualities we look for, Valentina.

"Both an unwavering sense of right and wrong, and a willingness to do what's necessary when right is threatened. Your first meeting with Blair, you weren't intimidated or cowed. Nor were you willing to be dragged into petty sniping. You know who you are and see no need to prove yourself to anyone. You rose to every physical challenge. Passed the psychological test—though you did not know that's what it was. And, you failed the initiation."

I started. "Wait? Failed the initiation? That's one of the criteria?"

Kessler laughed. "Of course it is. Revealing secrets under pressure? Can you imagine a worse quality in a spy? Naturally everyone who read the card to get into the sorority was excluded."

"But then, how? You only recruit Sams and Sallys, and you have to pass to become one?"

"You didn't."

My mouth opened and nothing came out.

"Exactly. You lied and gave a secret that wasn't on the card. So did Aiden, Leighton, Sawyer, Teagan, and others before them."

"But Ezra didn't read his secret either. He was kicked out."

"Ah." An uncomfortable look crossed her face. "Ezra Lennox was a good candidate on paper. Unfortunately, he failed the psychological test. I'm not saying he's dangerous, but he exhibited sociopathic tendencies that excluded him. Coupled with his witnessing Sawyer taken. It was an easy choice for Aiden to kick him out."

Sociopathic tendencies. Like what Ezra, Maverick, Ryder, and Jaxson did to Logan's cousin that night. Like how easily we tortured Aiden and Jade to find Maverick. I guess we are a bit sociopathic in defense of our family.

"No need to look so apologetic," I said. "Those tendencies are one of the things I love about him."

"Indeed." Kessler made for the door. "Will you walk with me now?"

I hesitated—but only for a moment.

We stepped outside and the world opened up on rolling hills and stretching trees. Wooden structures dotted the horizon—eerily similar to the obstacle course I ran as a pledge. There were more cabins on either side and in front of me. In the distance, a grand wooden building stood high, towering the horizon, and running past it was a group of twelve—all neat in rows of fours.

"Maverick." I lurched forward.

"He's not with them," Kessler said. "He's in the hall finishing an assignment like I said. This is his bunkhouse. He knows to meet us here after the tour." She set off down the steps. "Are you coming?"

Am I?

I looked toward what I assumed was the hall. Barging in there screaming his name might get me forcibly removed for all I knew. If Maverick really was coming to me when this was over, I could play along for a little longer.

"Are they all training for the program?" I asked, falling in step with her.

"They are."

I pulled a face. "They can't all be Sallys and Sams. Everyone would have noticed twelve brothers and sisters going missing."

"We've expanded in the last decade. We have chapters in universities throughout the country. They don't all call themselves Sams and Sallys, but they're held to the same standards that formed Zeta Rho."

"Why did you bring me here? You could've tackled me in your office, taken my phone, and had Aiden send the virus."

She chuckled. "My tackling days are behind me, Valentina. Besides, your boyfriend owns a media conglomerate. Your threats to go public with information carry more weight than most."

Smart woman, I thought. *I definitely would've followed through on revealing the program if she didn't take me to Maverick. Video or no video.*

"That said, we were overdue for a talk," she continued. "Your changes have affected recruitment. We need things to go back the way they were, but telling you so or trying to force it would've resulted in you pushing harder and demanding to know why. I say this affectionately: you've become a massive pain in my ass."

I barked a laugh. "You kidnapped my boyfriend and Aiden threatened Ezra. What did you expect?"

"I admit things have gotten out of control. It's natural for you all to question after being put through the initiation. How did we find that information? Are we spying on you—"

"Are you?" I sliced in. "How did you find out what was written on the card?"

"What happened in Evergreen Academy isn't as hidden as you believe. We dug into the incident when we dug into you. Miss Evergreen was very upfront about reacting in self-defense after you murdered her sister."

"That's a lie! Scarlett's death was an accident."

Kessler squeezed my arm. "I know. Miss Evergreen is exactly where she belongs. Still, this demonstrates that some mysteries are incredibly simple. One fraternity president with superior hacking skills, and another sorority president sitting down for a chat with an inmate. That's how all the secrets were gathered. It's natural for you to question how and dig into the truth behind the Sally house. We're prepared for those questions.

"What we weren't prepared for was Ezra seeing Sawyer taken. We weren't prepared for you to use the fundraiser as a ruse to unearth members of the program. We weren't prepared for you to become president and change the rules. We also weren't prepared for Aiden to recruit Maverick.

"And of course as a result, you were even more determined to unearth the big secret and sicced a formidable opponent against us. Marcus Beaumont used every resource at his disposal to find his son, and he did."

I stopped dead. "Excuse me? He did?"

"Yes, he did. Marcus is close personal friends with most of the people who sign our checks. He found Maverick and ended up bound to the same secrecy that prevented him telling you. Didn't you notice he hasn't made any progress?"

"Yes," I said, "but I figured he was running up against the same roadblocks I was. I didn't guess you were forcing everyone in my life to lie to me. And you call me a pain in the ass."

It was probably a good thing Kessler found me amusing instead of insulting.

"Well, our lies were in vain, weren't they? Maverick found his way back to you, and you found your way to him." She turned on me, smiling. "You are as impressive as advertised."

"Thank you, but if this compliment is on the heels of an offer to join you, let me give my rejection right now. There was no reason to put my family through this. No reason for my son to go to sleep crying for his father. You could've told me the truth from the beginning."

"It's not that simple, and if you put aside your anger for a moment, I think you'll see that." She grasped my shoulders. "First and foremost, it's mandated that *no one* can reveal their place in the program to anyone other than a spouse. Not even their parents. While I've no doubt about your devotion to one another, you are not Maverick's wife. We saw no reason to bend the rules for you both.

"Finally, and most important, Leighton Lewis. Leighton killed that man to avenge you. You were there that night, and although they swore you didn't know what they would do, you already have one death in your history."

More than one.

"I had to be certain you weren't another version of Leighton. For all I knew, you led the march to Logan's dorm room to slit his throat. Could I have blamed you? Absolutely not. I can't say I wouldn't have done the same thing if he attacked me while lying in wait to rape my best friend. But while your involvement would be understandable, it'd also exclude you from being in the program. We can't afford to train serial killers."

I flinched. Said so bluntly, her words did penetrate my anger. Why would they tell me about a top secret program when they didn't know they could trust me?

"All right," I said, choosing my words carefully. "Let's say I understand. What happens now?"

"You wouldn't have to be an active member of the program. I understand you hope to be a therapist. That's not a position we look for. What I really need from you, Valentina, is to return to the original program. Pledges have to be put through rigorous training. They need to do the initiation."

I shook my head. "I ran on the promise that I'd do away with that stuff. How would it look if I went *never mind* and brought it all back? The sisters would vote me out."

"I can make it simple for you. I'll update the charter to state these practices are mandatory. I'll be the bad guy, not you. Honestly, I could do that anyway, but I'm seeing the value in working *with* you. There are a lot less headaches that way."

"I don't know," I said, gazing around. "This is a lot to process in thirty minutes. None of this negates the fact that Aiden exhibits a few sociopathic tendencies of his own, and I'm seventy percent certain Leighton managed to survive the car crash. I'm sure you have good intentions here, but so far, the members of your program have lied to, threatened, attacked, drowned, and called me crazy."

She held up her hands. "Okay, okay. I understand that you haven't received the best picture of what we do. Come with me. Let me show you around and properly explain the program. Afterward, talk it over with Maverick."

I noticed how comfortable she was calling him by his first name.

"I would prefer it if we worked together from here on, Valentina. For the first time since this all began, I'm giving you a choice."

"I'll consider it," I replied after a long pause. "Please, commence with the tour. I've been after the truth for three years. I won't say no to more information."

Mrs. Kessler took me around what she called "the farm." I wasn't getting another name. Even so, I was certain we were still in the state. Not only in the state, but at most a few hours away from home. If it had been more than a five-hour drive, I'd be starving. As it was, my stomach didn't twinge, and the sun was just peeking its way to the highest point in the sky.

A couple of hours away and sitting on acres of fenced-in land, the farm held more than my initial look gave away. There was a running path and a fully equipped gym. Classrooms, a dining hall, library, laboratory, and a rec room. Everything was well-maintained and well-funded. My love was held against his will, but he wasn't held in squalor.

"What do they do here? How long does the training last?"

"It depends on the individual. Maverick is here to enhance his computers skills and build upon the talents that'll keep our government systems impregnable. There is physical training they all have to participate in, and that's a minimum of three months. With the tech training on top, Maverick is here for six months."

"Six? You were going to keep him here with a nonsense story about needing time off for six months?"

"We do what we have to."

I blew out a breath, shaking my head at the cavernous library we stood in. "All of this is hard to take. I'm trying to understand, but I can't wrap my head around it. To think a couple of freshmen make the choice to rush a fraternity, and then their whole life is turned upside down."

"The very fact that they chose Zeta Rho and Nu Alpha is proof they were looking for a different kind of life. You're not men and women who choose what is easy. You look to your future. You focus on building yourself and others up in every way, every day," Kessler said. "We're not looking for drones. We seek strong, compassionate people who aim to do what's right. I think you're one of those people, Valentina."

"Don't try to butter me up," I mumbled.

She laughed. "You must be tired of hearing me ramble on. Maverick should be heading back to the bunkhouse now. Do you need me to show you—?"

I was already out the door and racing across the grass. I counted the steps from Maverick's bunk. I did not need her to show me the way.

Ahead of me, a group of people broke apart in front of the bunkhouses, and one figure in particular veered right. I knew that build and back of the head better than I did my own.

Maverick went inside and shut the door.

"Maverick!" I burst in.

He spun, catching me when I jumped. "Val!"

The force knocked him back onto the bed. Which was just as well.

I tore at his clothes—kissing him all over and sobbing about how much I missed him.

"I'm so sorry," he said. Maverick gripped the back of my neck, smashing our lips together, flipping me over. "I missed you so much. I love you."

We went at it like wild beasts. My screams were loud enough his roommates should've known not to come in. But we got one "Oh, shit!" and a slammed door that didn't stop us.

Maverick kissed a burning trail up my stomach. I could see the imprint of his lips in my cooling sweat. "Don't you ever do that to me again," I murmured, running my fingers over his new buzz cut.

"I didn't exactly ask to be drugged and thrown in the back of a van." He nipped the sensitive skin under my nipple. "But I'm sorry either way. Coming here wasn't my choice. Staying was. If it helps, I argued with my handler every day to let me call and tell you what was going on. You're my wife in every way that matters."

I bit my lip, not wanting to smile at him when I was supposed to be angry. My heart warmed anyway.

"They told you no and you still found a way, Maverick. That's what matters to me." I cradled his head to my chest. "Why did you stay? Was it just to nerd out over computers?"

He laughed. "There's more to it than that. The kind of work they're training me for... Val, Maverick Tech would have an exclusive relationship with the government. Every contract. All of their systems from the White House to the NSA. This is huge for us. My dad's drunk from all the champagne he's been popping in celebration."

"So, you do want this?"

He grinned into my eyes. "I do. My only regrets are what our family has been going through, and that George just saw more of my ass than he ever wanted to. This bunkhouse thing does not work for me."

I cracked up. "No doubt, I did imagine more privacy for our re-union. Does this mean you're staying for the full six months?"

"The dean is an alumnus of the program. That's why the many disappearances over the years were brushed off. She arranged for my classes to be taken online and exams given here at the farm. It's all set up so I can fit seamlessly back into my life like nothing happened." He stroked my cheek. "But I'm not like the other coeds who came here with no attachments and nothing to lose. We make this decision together. Should I stay? Should you join?"

Leaning back, I gazed up at the ceiling. "This program has made our lives hell for the last three years. How can I put all that aside for one speech and a tour?"

"Then, we won't." Maverick pushed himself up. "I'll pack my things now."

"Baby." I gently lowered him on top of me. "I know you. You want to be here, don't you? This is Christmas for you. Talking tech all day long. Learning things you could never learn in the classroom. I can't rip you out of here if it's where you want to be."

"With you is where I want to be, Val. Say the word," he whispered. "And we'll go home."

I thought about it. For a long time, I thought.

"What do you say?" he asked.

I opened my mouth, and gave my answer.

Chapter Nine

"Goodbye, Valentina."

"Goodbye." I climbed out of the car and watched Mrs. Kessler drive off. When her car rounded the corner, I knocked on Aiden's door.

He answered with a pleasant look that vanished at the sight of me. "What do you want? It's done. The virus shredded through your computers like paper."

"That's not why I'm here, though you're still a jerk for that. I came to give you this." I tossed him the keys. "The car. It's yours."

Aiden looked from me to the keys, eyes wide. "What?"

"You're not who I thought you were. I was right about you being an asshole... but wrong about the rest. I'm sorry for electrocuting you till you wet yourself."

"That was sweat!"

"But you did kidnap my boyfriend, so this makes us even."

"Getting your boyfriend in on the biggest opportunity of his life does not equate to torture," Aiden snapped. "Damn. You really suck at apologies, don't you?"

"I just gave you a four-million-dollar car. I don't suck that much."

Aiden's brows blew up his head. "Four million? Seriously?"

"Seriously. And also seriously, I'm sorry. I went too far that night. My only defense is I truly believed Maverick was in danger."

"I understand why you thought that." Sounded like the words were pulled from him. "I didn't give a great impression of a good guy when

I threatened to tell the Sons of Slaughter where Ezra's brother was hiding. I wouldn't have, by the way. It was a bluff to get him to back off."

"I know that now."

"Do you?" he asked, cocking his head. "Know everything?"

I nodded.

"So, are we working together or what, Moon?"

"Those are my options now. Keep my position as president and return Zeta Rho to how it was, or leave Somerset so my replacement can put the sisters back to work. Is it worth it?"

"We're molding the people who are going to protect and change this country, Valentina. How could it not be?"

I didn't reply.

"Since I'm out a car, mind giving me a ride? I've got one more person to apologize to."

Grinning, he tossed the keys in the air. "Sure."

"I'll have my phone back while you're at it."

Aiden drove me to campus. It was still winter break, so the house was nearly empty. Jade was the only one to answer my call when I asked if anyone was home.

"Valentina."

She didn't look up from the tomatoes she was chopping. Taking a seat on the stool, I slid across a salted caramel pretzel cupcake.

"I noticed you ate three the last time I bought some."

"Why are you giving me this?"

"I was hoping it'd be the first kind gesture of our new start," I said. "You were right, I didn't understand what you or the Sallys were here to do. I'm sorry for what we did to you that night."

"Understand what we're here to do?" she repeated. "What exactly do you understand?"

"Mrs. Kessler took me on a trip, and we had a long talk. I know where Maverick is and why."

Jade swept the tomatoes into a bowl. She still wasn't looking at me. "I'm pleased to hear it. Must be a relief to know he's safe."

"It is. Safe and happy where he is."

"What does this change between you and me, Valentina? You've painted me as the enemy. Tortured me like one too. How many cupcakes would it take to overcome that?"

"You tortured someone too."

Jade stilled.

"Came at them relentlessly until they saw no way out. All for someone you loved. I thought Maverick needed me, so I did what I thought I had to do. If anyone understands, it's you."

Meeting my eyes, Jade studied me with an expression I couldn't name.

"I accepted," I continued. "I'm continuing what the first Sally and her mother started. Means I'll need you to be the bad guy who announces you pushed for things to go back the way they were and Kessler listened. I'll take the blame, though. Say it's my fault for changing things too fast. We'll start over, go slow, and find a way to improve the process for choosing candidates."

"We?"

"Blair doesn't know about the program, so I'll rely on you to help me assess the sisters. Together we'll continue the good work that's done here, and do away with the screwed-up shit like drugging and kidnapping. There's a better way to recruit candidates."

"And the initiation?"

She was talking to me. Asking questions. This was a start.

"As much as I hate to admit it, the test is effective," I forced out. "What better way to find out if someone will reveal a deep secret under pressure than to do just that? Even so, there has to be another way. We're entitled to our secrets, Jade."

"If you have suggestions, let's hear them."

"Do you want to hear them? Are we working together?"

Sighing, Jade pushed her salad away. "I came here to work with you, Val. It didn't seem that way at first, and in many ways, I went too far too. You were terrified for your boyfriend and knew everyone around you was lying. That would make even the most sensible person desperate. It won't be right away," she said firmly. "But you and I can get to a point that we trust each other. It will mean being flexible—for both of us. And it will mean being rigid no matter how much the sisters complain about going back to the old ways. Which they will.

"The Sally house has always had one goal," she said. "It's not partying, sleepovers, or sisterhood. But it is about making a difference. If that can be enough for you—" Jade held out her hand. "We'll have no problem working together."

I shook. "I'm ready. Why wouldn't I be? Like I said, everyone's going to blame you."

She chuckled. "Come over here and get started on that fajita-stuffed chicken you made last month. Now that will go a long way toward me forgiving you."

"One fajita-stuffed chicken with a side of guac coming up."

RYDER

Valentina trudged into our bedroom that night, looking like she was about to drop on our bed and sleep for a year.

"How'd it go?" I asked.

"You're out a Lamborghini."

I shrugged. "I've got two more. Come here."

Valentina collapsed on top of me, squeezing tight. "This whole thing is a mess, Ryder."

"At least you're both safe. But if you could expound on your last couple texts, that would be great."

Val texted me earlier saying Mrs. Kessler gave in to her demands and brought her to Maverick. Even bigger news than our laptops and computers turning into useless blocks of metal and plastic. She said she couldn't talk right then because she was with Aiden Connelly of all people, and she'd tell us more when she got home. The main headline was she and Maverick were safe.

"Where is he? What's going on?"

Val propped her chin on my chest. "Legally, I'm not allowed to tell you unless we're married. Now would be a good time to put a ring on this finger."

I gaped at her.

Valentina burst out laughing. "I'm kidding. Well, not about the half a dozen legal documents I signed, but I am kidding about letting them stop me. We should get Ezra and Jaxson in here for this. The truth is even crazier than fiction."

"Before we do," I said, stopping her getting up. "You should know... I found my father. Or at least the man I think is my father."

"What? Ryder."

She cupped my cheeks and I gently drew her arms away. I didn't need comforting. I wasn't breaking down or sobbing inside a little hole in my heart.

"This is him." I showed her the photos I found online.

"Wow," she breathed. "Ryder, you look just like him. I'm so glad you'll still have your hair in twenty years."

I cracked a grin, appreciating the attempt to lighten the mood.

"What are you thinking?"

"Everything. Nothing," I said. "Every time I look at him, I hear my mom in my head. She made her choices to give her family a future, and now this guy has one of his own." I swiped through the photos, landing on one with the same woman and three kids. "Just meeting him could bring both our lives crashing down around us. Mom's and mine for sure."

"Did Caroline flatly state that he doesn't know about you?" Val stretched out by my side. "Maybe he does and they both agreed it was best he keep his distance."

"Maybe. I'm not sure what'll happen if I start another conversation about it. Mom was clear that door is closed."

"You didn't know who he was then. You didn't have a name." A light kiss tickled my cheek. "Caroline is in full-mama-bear mode. It's hard for her to see past her need to protect. Try again. Make her see that you two must have this conversation."

"We do need to. I won't be this calm about it forever, but if I'm honest, all I really feel right now is relief."

"Relief?"

It was my turn to cup her cheek. "Relief no part of me is Benjamin Shea. Relief that Charles Nelson is still out there and there's a chance to get to know him if I choose to. Relief there's no longer this question mark hanging over my head." I made a noise in my throat. "How embarrassing will it be if he isn't the guy and I'm swiping on some random?"

"There's no way this man isn't related to you," Val said. "If he's not your father, then he's your father's identical twin." Val zoomed in on the photos. "They must be your brothers and sister. This man's genes are strong. None of you stood a chance. Good thing he's handsome."

"You're not about to develop another dad crush, are you?"

"I do not have a crush on Jaxson's dad! I make one joke years ago and I cannot live it down."

I tackled her shrieking into the pillows, going at her buttons. "Story time. I want to know exactly what happened today, and you don't need to be wearing clothes while you tell me."

Giggling, she tried to roll away from me. I pinned her to the mattress, keeping Val where she belonged.

"It's a long conversation, baby."

I did away with her pants.

"It all started with Sally Hollenbeck..."

VALENTINA

"What are you feeling today? Eggs or oatmeal?"

"Oatmeal with chocolate chips and cinnamon," Adam said.

I smooched his cheek. "You know Chef would never let you have all that sweet stuff first thing in the morning."

He pressed a finger to his lips. "Shh. Don't tell her, Mommy."

"It's our little secret," I said. "You can have all the chocolate and cinnamon you want. Matter of fact, why don't we take these ingredients and make cinnamon chocolate chip oatmeal cookies?"

Adam about fell off his chair. "Cookies for breakfast?"

"I won't tell if you don't."

"Yay! I'll get Alba."

Adam ran off to get his giraffe and I looked up the rest of what we'd need. Of course, I'd be a responsible mom and give him a bowl of fruit or something to go with the cookies, but I was in so good a mood, I didn't care how many varieties of stink eye I'd get from Chef for upsetting the perfectly balanced diets she arranged for us.

With my inclusion into the program, Maverick was allowed to program another number on his phone. We talked every night around when I put Adam to bed. He got a chance to say good night to our son, and then the rest of the time we talked about what he was learning, and all the things he'd do to me when he got home. I still missed him so much it was a daily physical ache in my side. But knowing he was safe and doing what he loved made it okay.

All of my guys were safe and in better positions than we were three years ago, when we set foot on Somerset campus with naïve dreams of pretending our problems would go away if we became different people.

Ezra wasn't in a rush to forgive Aiden kicking off the events that got him tangled with a violent New York gang and shot. Even so, Ezra putting himself in harm's way like that, woke Brian up to the brother he was ignoring. It brought the entire family closer in the way they wanted to be, but could never quite achieve.

Jaxson's internship at Interstellar started off rocky. Now his father considered him essential. They worked together. Made decisions together. Argued over the next bands to sign together. Jaxson had long since proved himself to a certain business partner, and things were as good at work as they were at home. Especially since we all got to see him more often.

As for my Ryder, it had been a week since he found Charles Nelson online. A week he'd been considering what to do with the distraction of classes starting, and his girlfriend and brother joining a top secret government program that recruits bright young people headed into the private sector for partnerships with the CIA, NSA, DOD and more. That's a lot to deal with when you're struggling over the question of meeting your long-lost father.

"Morning." Ryder came into the kitchen and kissed me on the way to the coffee pot. "Adam says we're having cookies for breakfast?"

"My boy doesn't lie," I sang.

"What's the occasion?"

"I'm happy." I hugged him from behind. "Why can't I be crazily, wildly happy when I'm in love with four sexy, wonderful guys and we're about to start a new chapter on Monday without all the fear that's gripped us for the last three years?"

"You can be as happy as you want, Moon." He twisted to soften the words with a kiss. "I've still got Jacob digging up everything he can find on the Kessler woman and her little program."

"She didn't create it," I said. "I don't think she runs it either."

"She wouldn't tell you if she did."

I nodded, pushing out my lips. "Good point."

"How are you so accepting of this?"

"I trust Maverick's judgment."

Ryder snorted. "That's because you haven't known him as long as I have. He's the same guy that found a hurt bobcat in the woods, and tried to nurse him back to health under his bed. I wish you hadn't signed those papers before I looked at them."

"They weren't exactly giving me the option of running home to go over it with my lawyers. I wasn't supposed to tell you at all."

"Another thing that pisses me off."

"Rightly so. That's why it's a good thing I'd never keep the truth from you."

"Promise me that—"

"—I'll tell you if it gets too much or things begin to feel off again? I will." I went back to the ingredients destined to become cookies. "My part in this is small anyway. I assess the Sallys for the best candidates like Aiden does with the Sams. That's all."

"I still don't trust this Aiden guy. He's twisted. Obviously he faked his way through the psychology test, because if anyone's got sociopathic tendencies, it's him."

"Aiden graduates this semester. We won't have to worry about him in a few months." I eyed him. "What about you? Have you made a decision yet?"

"Part of me thinks I should talk to Mom before I do anything. Even though she shut me down the first time, it'd be nice to know if Charles knows I exist. Either he agreed to have nothing to do with me, or he doesn't know me. Either way my showing up won't be a happy surprise."

"Don't say that. Of course he'd be happy to see you. You're his son."

"A son he hasn't seen for twenty-one years. If he didn't know about me, can you imagine how hard it'd be to find out you missed that much of your kid's life?"

"It will be hard," I said softly. "And messy. And frustrating. And all the things in between. That's what family is, Ryder. But if I can give my opinion...?"

He nodded.

"When you were born, your mom had every reason to be afraid of the abusive husband who held your and your family's future hostage. Benjamin is gone now, and so is any power he had over you. Even if the world finds out you're not entitled to the inheritance, you have family and friends who'll make sure you, your mom, and her family will want for nothing. I'd also like to point out the rightful heir would never sue you."

Ryder cracked a smile as said rightful heir ran in carrying his giraffe.

"For once, you can be selfish, baby. He's your father. This is your life and your relationship with him. You get to decide."

"You always know what to say." Ryder kissed me slow and sweet—skimming my bottom lip till I opened and welcomed the deep probing of our melded tongues.

"Ewww."

"I'll show you ew." Ryder chased him out the kitchen.

"Careful," I called.

I got to work making the dough and then laying it out on the pan. My phone rang as I was putting them in the oven. Jade flashed on the screen.

"Hi, Jade."

"Hello," she said. "Is now a good time to talk?"

"Yeah. What's up?"

"I was hoping you could come over to the house today. We didn't finish ironing out the details for the test you're giving the new sisters in place of the initiation. Mrs. Kessler would like to know exactly how you'll make it work."

"Um." I checked the time. "I'm making breakfast now, and then I'm taking Adam to see his favorite godmother. I could leave them to hang out and come around one. Is that good?"

"Perfect. Thank you."

Jade hung up.

I let the cookies do their thing in the oven, and began chopping up pineapples, apples, bananas, and kiwi for a fruit salad. Ezra came in and threw himself in a chair.

"How'd it go?" I asked.

"Recovered and sent. You're looking at a man who will not fail his journalism assignment and bring shame on his family name."

"That's great, love. Sorry again about the virus."

"It's not your fault. It's just another thing Aiden's going to square with me the next time we meet up."

Yeah, Ezra was a long way from forgiveness. I couldn't blame him.

"Adam and I are going to Sofia's after breakfast, then I'm running over to the Sally house. Will you pick him up if I'm running late?"

"Why? What's up?"

"Jade wants to go over my new plan for the initiation. I get that it's a good test to see how well the sisters can keep a secret, but I'm not digging through anyone's past for amateur porn videos and fifty-year-old boyfriends."

"I'd like more details on that, please."

"Tough," I teased, straddling his lap. "So, will you?"

"Sure. My project is done. How about I go with you? The last time Sofia and I hung out, we were…"

Torturing my housemother and brother president for information.

"This time we'll just make things explode in the backyard. She bought Adam a little chemistry set."

"I'd like to see that."

A few hours later, I left Adam, Sofia, and Ezra making baking soda volcanoes and hopped in the car to Somerset. I didn't mind sitting down with Jade to talk plans. I didn't have all the details worked out, but I liked my idea for the new initiation.

Kessler said Zeta Rho's priority wasn't sisterhood. To me that was because no one else was willing to question the system and fight to make it so. If they wanted more of that, they should've chosen another president.

I parked on Greek Row directly in front of the Sally house. Classes started on Monday, but campus didn't officially open until tomorrow, Saturday. In twenty-four hours, I'd be fighting to get parking in front of my house.

"Hello?" I pushed inside, shutting the door behind me. "Jade?"

Setting my bag down, I peeked my head in the kitchen, saw no one, and continued upstairs. Her door hung open.

"Jade?"

I shoved on the wood, letting it swing in. I saw the pool of red first.

"Jade!"

I tripped on her yoga mat running in, and landed on my knees beside her. A nasty wound gushed blood from her temple. It drained the color from her skin, leaving her so pale it appeared she was dead. Only the shuddering rise and fall of her chest promised me otherwise.

"Jade," I cried. "What happened? Who did—?"

The floorboard creaked.

I whipped around just as the red mass flew at me. I threw myself to the side, screaming as pain exploded in my thigh. Reacting on instinct, I kicked out and connected.

"Argh!"

The figure staggered and a wisp of reddish-gold hair escaped the hood. It was the last thing I saw before they straightened and lifted the fire extinguisher again.

I rolled out of the way.

Bang!

My heart leapt in my throat as the floor splintered where I'd just been.

"Stop!"

"Stay still!"

Recognition almost stilled me like she wanted. I knew that voice.

Heaving the red metal canister, she towered over me—light illuminating the hatred etched in her face.

There!

A stack of dumbbells claimed space by Jade's dresser. I grabbed and swung as she did. A deafening clang resounded in my ears—as loud as her scream.

She dropped the fire extinguisher, clutching the hand smashed by the eight-pound weight, and it landed on me. The air punched out of my stomach.

I gasped, wheezing for air and receiving none.

"Bitch!" she shrieked. Blood dripped from her clutched hands. "Look what you did!"

What I did?! But I couldn't say it. I couldn't catch my breath to speak at all.

"Why won't you die?"

"Why... should I?" I gasped. "Reagan."

"You're dangerous. You'll destroy everything and no one sees it!"

"What the hell are you talking about!"

Her lips twisted. It's a wonder I recognized her, because the woman with the brunette bob and pierced lip was long gone. Ratty, greasy locks were dyed the same shade as Leighton's. The piercing was gone, and all that adorned her lips was cashmere brown lipstick—also familiar.

"Don't pretend you don't know. Just won't drop the innocent act."

I stared at her in disbelief. I haven't seen Reagan since freshman year, and now she was here swinging fire extinguishers like she'd undoubtedly done to Jade.

"Don't do that," she hissed. "Don't look at me like I'm crazy."

I moved as Reagan moved. She grabbed the weight and I the dresser, yanking out the scissors.

"That's enough." Pushing myself up, I brandished my weapon. "Whatever you think your problem is with me, you're wrong. I haven't seen you for years, Reagan, and before that, we barely had anything to do with each other."

"Didn't have anything to do with each other?" Reagan ripped the hoodie off. "I killed a man to protect you and your worthless friend."

My body trembled. "I didn't ask you to do that."

"You didn't have to. Leighton was there for you. She refused to let anyone hurt you, or get away with it. For her number one recruit, we killed Logan Bilius, and what was our reward?" She raised the weight, holding it on me as though it was a gun. "We were thrown out. Out of the Sallys. Out of Zeta. Out of the program!"

"Is that what this is about?" Shock nearly stole my voice again. "Are you serious? I didn't ask for that either. I wanted to call the police. Killing him was your choice. Whatever came after was your choice too."

"My choice?" Reagan scoffed. "You still don't get it, and you never will. There was no choice. Leighton said we had to stop him from hurting anyone else, so that's what we did. I obey orders, Moon. I do what I'm told. *You*," she spat. "You're a useless, slutty piece of trash who was supposed to blow out of here in four years, and then a real president would take over. All the damage you were doing would be corrected, so we should just wait you out."

"Wait for what? What does any of this have to do with you? Your ass was thrown out."

"Ahh!"

Reagan threw the weight. I ducked and it went sailing over my head, smashing through the window.

My heart hammered in my chest like a caged animal. I dug my palm in my breastbone. *You're not the only one who wants out of here.*

"I can't be fired from my duty to my country. Leighton chose us— She chose you because we're meant to make a difference. She was the b-best person." Reagan's voice cracked. "And she died in disgrace because of you."

Died? I thought. *Leighton truly is dead, and the phantoms I've been seeing—the shadow hanging over my head.*

I gazed in her hate-filled eyes.

Was her.

"I didn't want that," I said softly. "I didn't ask Leighton to do what you guys did, but I appreciated it all the same. The world didn't mourn the death of one more rapist. I for fuck sure didn't."

"No, what you wanted was to undo all of Leighton's hard work. She and the Sallys who came before. Don't try to lie," she snapped when I opened my mouth. "I've watched you, Moon. After Leighton died, I didn't know what to do until I realized you were to blame. I came back to find you surrounded by bodyguards. I couldn't get close."

A shiver scaled my spine. How long has Reagan been following me?

"I convinced those in the house still loyal to Leighton to watch you. Tell me when there was an opening. Teagan convinced me you weren't worth it." Reagan picked up another weight. "You were causing so much trouble, you were bound to be thrown out too. It was only a matter of time before the problem would take care of itself, so why dirty my hands in your filthy blood?"

My lips peeled back of their own volition. Where did she get off talking to me this way? Hating me for decisions I had no control over. "How was I supposed to know there was a program to be kicked out of? I was doing what I thought I had to. I know differently now. Things have changed."

"I know," she hissed. "Teagan told me you signed the contract. You're the newest member of the Hollenbeck program. That was some impressive trick you pulled—convincing Kessler you're trustworthy and happy to be part of the team now."

"I am both of those things."

"You're a liar. Ungrateful, smug, rich bitch liar." She moved fast.

The weight flew at my head. I lurched to the side, swallowing a screech at the dent in the plaster. There was no doubt Reagan was aiming to kill.

"I've waited so long for *you* to get what you gave Leighton! Kicked out of school and forced to leave your family for some backwater community college hellhole until the day you had a little accident. But it never happened."

"Reagan, please." I wasn't entertaining this nonsense anymore. Jade was bleeding out on the carpet. I had to do something now. "I can't imagine how hard it was to lose Somerset and then your best friend. I understand that you needed someone to blame—"

"You're to blame." She took a step toward me and I moved to the side, hugging the wall. "I figured out the truth of what you were doing when I followed you to St. Germaine. You attacked Aiden. Nearly drowned him. He honored your worthless boyfriend by giving him a place in the program, and that's how you repaid him."

"I didn't know about the program!" Frustration made my voice a screech.

"Didn't you? With all your money, bodyguards, companies, and hackers? You knew all along." She took another step. Then another. "You want to destroy us, and no one sees it but me. I tried to kill you outside Kessler's building."

I rocked back, mouth falling open.

"I tried again when you somehow tracked Aiden's new place down. Then, he called for you." Reagan tossed her head. "He wasn't surprised to see you. Somehow, you got your hooks in him and Kessler. I don't care how. Whatever lies you told them won't work on me."

Reagan picked up Jade's resistance band, and drew it tight. "I'm getting rid of you once and for all."

I eyed her, backing slowly toward the door. "This isn't going to go the way you want, Reagan. You're not in the mood to listen to me, but you should hear this: you won't kill me."

"You think I'm not capable?"

"No, you're a killer," I stated. "It's as plain as the blue in your eyes. It's not that you can't kill me, it's that you won't. That's not how this ends." I stopped moving and took my stance. "What's going to happen is either you put that down and let me get you some help, or I'm going to kick your insane stalker ass all over this room."

"I'd like to see that."

"You will. If you're stupid enough to go with option two."

Reagan lunged at me before the end of the sentence.

We collapsed in a heap of flailing limbs. Reagan struggled to pin me down. Wrap the band around my neck. She jammed her knee brutally between my shoulder, forced the band under my head, and pulled tight.

My hand cut through the air, and sunk the scissors in her right thigh. Reagan's scream shattered Greek Row.

Using the distraction, I backhanded her, knocking the madwoman off of me. She fell off and almost took my head with her.

The band snapped me up and released as it slid off. I banged back on the floor, dazed.

Get up, Valentina. Up!

I shoved up on my feet—hands as bloody as hers. Reagan limped a fair distance away from me. I saw in her eyes she was reevaluating how easy a target I was.

That was not good.

As long as it was since we lived in the same house, I remember clearly how active, adept, and merciless she was. Reagan exceeded her physical requirements, and attended martial arts classes on the weekends.

I had to keep her off-balance. Expose her weakness before she found mine.

"What do you think you're going to accomplish?" I flung. "All this time you've been watching me. Stalking me. For what? Leighton's still dead. You're still out of the program."

"I'm *protecting* the program. I'm standing up for what's right like Leighton did, and Sally Hollenbeck before her." Reagan planted her feet, raising her arms up. "They'll throw me a parade when you're gone. I'll be welcomed back, and then I can start the work of returning the Sally house to how it should be."

"You're stuck three years in the past. You can't see the Sallys moved on. Leighton moved on." I narrowed on her. "The package you left for me on Leighton's bed. Did you look inside? Do you know what was in there?"

"What does that have to do with anything? Stop talking," she snapped. "You were bragging about kicking my ass. Let's see it, Moon."

"The knife was in the package," I plowed on.

"What?" Reagan lowered her fists a fraction. "That's not true."

I seized on her shock. "It is true. If Leighton hated me and was so angry and vengeful, why didn't she mail it to the police instead of making sure it came back to me? Leighton didn't want me gone. She didn't hate me. You may think you're doing this in her name, but it's all about you."

"You're lying, Moon." Reagan's fists came right back up. "Leighton told me that package held exactly what you deserved. All these years I've imagined it was a pile of dog shit. Now, I told you to stop talking. You open your mouth to spew more garbage about Leighton, and you'll die slow like this traitor."

She kicked Jade.

"Don't touch her!" Reaching behind, I grabbed a heavy candle and lobbed it at her head. Reagan ducked to avoid it and I ran at her, swinging for her nose.

Reagan dodged the punch, but rebounded quick—striking me in the gut. I doubled over, dropping the scissors. She clutched my head and smashed her knee in my face. The pain was blinding.

She shoved me stumbling over Jade onto the mattress. I came to as she lunged for me and kicked up. My sneaker smashed her jaw, snapping Reagan's head up like a PEZ dispenser.

"We don't have to do this," I shouted. "I want the same things, Reagan. I'll return the Sally house to how it was. I'm working *with* Aiden, Jade, and Kessler. The backhanded information you've been getting from Teagan is wrong."

"Argh!" She dove on the bed.

I rolled out of the way and thumped on the floor. "Let me talk to Kessler," I said, crawling to Jade.

I checked her pulse. Faint. Thready. But there.

"I'll convince her to let you back in."

Reagan climbed off the bed, rage stoking the glint in her eyes to flames. As unlikely and nonsensical as it was, I felt I was looking straight into the heart of madness. There was nothing I could say to stop her.

"I don't want to hurt you, Reagan," I said even as I accepted the truth. Even as she picked up the fallen scissors. "Please. It doesn't have to be this way."

"Yes, it does."

Reagan lunged at me, and the world came into sharp focus.

The beads of sweat glistening on her forehead. Her fingers dripping a trail of crimson leading to me. The curve of her lips twisting from contempt to glee. Scissors glinting silver and red in the sunlight.

She brought the weapon down. I closed around her wrist, taking the brunt of her weight like a freight train. I crashed against the windowsill—sharp pain buckled my spine.

"Die," she spat. "Die!" Reagan forced her fist down, the sharpened steel ever closer to my eye.

Muscles bulging. Veins popping. Both hands strained to keep her at bay, and were failing.

Centimeter by centimeter, her strength bested mine. I blinked and my lashes brushed the tip.

"Argh!" Desperation flooded all sense. I flung my head back. And the air didn't catch me.

A scream ripped from my throat as we fell out the window.

Reagan tumbled head over heels. She scrabbled for any part of me, snagged my shirt, and ripped it clean off. Her short cry ended with an abrupt, silencing thud.

I hung upside down—chest heaving. Body swaying above hers.

Something had a hold of my ankle. The hold that stopped me falling out.

Jade struggled to her feet, clamping down on my thighs. "Give me your hand." She helped me back in.

"Thank you. Thank you, thank you, thank you."

"No problem." Jade's head lolled. A dab of vomit on the corner of her mouth and the pile on the carpet said what she did before rescuing me. "Would you call me an ambulance now?"

Final Chapter

"I cannot apologize to you enough, Valentina." Ophelia Kessler stood in my living room. That would've been the oddest thing to happen that week if I wasn't nearly killed by a former sorority sister. "We had no idea Reagan left her school in Kansas, or that she was in contact with Teagan."

"Or that she was insane," Ryder barked. He held me tighter. "Did you print your fucking psych test from the back of a cereal box?"

"Again," she said evenly. "I apologize. In future, we will keep a much closer eye on former members of the program. Teagan will be disciplined, and Jade is receiving the best care at Evergreen General Hospital. They expect her to make a full recovery."

"How do we know this is over?" I asked. "What about Priscilla? Or the leftover members from Leighton's reign? What if they're playing rock-paper-scissors right now to see who'll come after me next?"

"We've checked on Priscilla and she is exactly where she should be six thousand miles away. More so, she's happily engaged and making plans to open a law firm with her future husband. She bears no ill will toward you, Leighton, or the program. She stated many times that getting out from under Leighton's influence was the best thing for her, and she appreciates that we gave her a new life instead of a jail cell. You have nothing to worry about with her."

"And the others?"

"They both say they didn't care for Leighton very much. You're the better president," she said. "I assure you, Val, the matter has been taken care of. But just in case, Jade will be coming back to keep an eye on things, along with the security team the dean hired to monitor Zeta Rho and Greek Row."

"We have security," Ezra said. "And they'll be sticking to you from now on till the end of time," he told me.

We'll have that discussion later.

"Thank you for coming," I said. "For giving us an update about Jade and for taking steps to make certain nothing like this happens again. My first impression of Leighton, Priscilla, and Reagan after Logan was that they were a cult. I see now how true that was, and how much of a hold Leighton had on them. Reagan couldn't reconcile her death. She needed someone to blame."

"That someone wasn't you." Jaxson kissed the back of my hand. "Whatever she told you, nothing that happened was your fault."

"I know," I said softly. "I also know I should be relieved she's gone and I'm safe again. But I just feel awful. So much of the last three years has been plagued by secrets, hate, revenge, and lies. Now someone has died for it."

Silence smothered us. No one knew what else to say. Least of all me.

"I'll leave you now." Kessler squeezed my shoulder. "But not with nothing. I will think about what you said. Changes must be made. I can't say what they'll be, but it's obvious we can't go on the way we have." She smiled. "Maybe you'll be the one who shows us a better path."

Ryder waited till she was out of the room. "Like fuck. You're out of that insane asylum starting yesterday. They can find someone else to recruit their basket cases."

"They're not all like that," I said. "Maverick said the people he's training with are a good bunch. I think in this case a leader with too much charisma slipped the net." I laced my fingers through his and Jaxson's. "What matters now is it's over. And if it's not, I will agree to security. I've got one more year of Somerset. Damned if I'm not making it to graduation after all I've survived."

Eight Months Later

"GOOD MORNING, PLEDGES."

"Good morning, Valentina."

I did away with the drill sergeant/cadet vibe the previous presidents went for. Even so, I'd be lying if I said I didn't like having my name chorused back at me from riveted faces.

"Now, you all know the reputation of Zeta Rho Sigma. It's why you chose to be here when you could be doing Jell-O shots off the Chi Psi Omegas."

They tittered.

"Don't get me wrong. We'll have a lot of fun this semester. There will be parties, cookouts, trips, and taking over the Nu Alpha's pool. But none of that is going to get in the way of us kicking ass in everything we do—like a true Zeta does."

"Whoo!" the ladies cheered.

"You're in for bonding activities, physical activities, and challenges of my own design to see who is the best fit for Zeta," I said. "Obviously, I wish that could be all of you, but in this case, whether or not you become a Zeta is up to you. It's on you to fulfill your requirements and show up every day to dominate."

Blair stepped up just as I put my hand out. She placed the cards on my palm.

"And it's on you to pass the test that will ultimately decide if you're accepted into the house." The pledges sat up straighter. "You can crush it in every other way, but if you do not make it through this, you cannot become a sister."

Rivka raised her hand. "What do we have to do?"

"On each of these cards I've written a single sentence. Each sentence different and each meant for one of you. Your task is simple. By the end of this semester, if I or one of the sisters get you to tell us what is written on your card, you're out."

The girls shared looks, shrugging and muttering to each other.

"That doesn't sound so bad."

I grinned. "It doesn't, does it?"

Their smiles dimmed.

"First off, no one is going to harm you physically or emotionally. But otherwise, anything goes in getting you to give up the information, and trust me, we're coming at you with everything we've got."

Not an exaggeration. Jade was skeptical my version of the initiation could work, so she had me do a test run last semester. All the sisters were given cards with the same rules, except I sweetened the pot by promising to pay for the winner's summer vacation trip to anywhere they wanted to go. By the end, only Sofia and Blair held on to their secrets, and they were still lording it over us.

Rightly so, it got intense. One weekend, Berkeley threw a surprise sangria party and everyone got plastered. She got six secrets out of drunk Zetas before anyone realized what she was doing. The ladies really dug deep into their most crafty, manipulative selves, and I couldn't be prouder.

Since the big secrets were nothing more than random history facts kept the game from having the six-week aftermath where everyone walked around in shame with their heads down. We were never going back to the old initiation—whether I was president or not.

"What do you say, ladies? Up for it?"

"Hell, yeah."

Laughing, I passed out the cards, catching Mai's thumbs-up across the room. After this, Sofia's boyfriend, Hudson, was throwing a party at his place to celebrate the start of our final year. She didn't know we were actually going to what would be her engagement party after Hudson proposed in front of their families and friends.

Mai's signal told me everyone was there and ready for us. All they needed was Sofia.

We shoved our shoes on in the hall after the meeting.

"It's not like Hudson to throw parties," Sofia remarked. "He must feel it too."

I threw big, panicked eyes at Mai. "Feel what?" I asked in what I hoped was a casual tone.

"That we finally did it. No more craziness. No more drama. We're going to have the fun, normal year at school we've waited for." She threw her arms around our shoulders. "Our senior year is going to kill. We're getting wild, ladies. I hope you're ready."

I laughed. "Damn straight. I'm feeling it too."

We got her in the car and drove the short distance to Hudson's apartment. My guys were already there—Maverick, Ezra, Jaxson, and Ryder—posted up in the corner drinking beers. I slid in between them.

"Hello, lovers."

"Hi." Ryder kissed me soft, unhurried, and too passionate for public.

"How did it go?" I whispered.

"Good. We went out to the beach house. Talked. Had a few beers," he said. "I invited Mom to join us. She came just as he was about to leave. But she came."

"I'm so proud of you."

I was. Ryder went back and forth on contacting his father. A month after finding him, he finally broached the topic with his mom—photo of Charles Nelson in hand. Caroline shut down any conversation about him, and that was the kick up my mercurial love's backside to pick up the phone.

In the years I'd known them, that was the first time I witnessed true conflict between Caroline and Ryder. She never told him Ryder existed, and the call she got from an angry, sorrowful Charles left her in tears. For a week, she and Ryder didn't speak to each other.

Ryder understood why she made that choice. Caroline was afraid of what Benjamin would do if he found out Ryder wasn't his son, and Ryder witnessed the consequences himself. Benjamin was beastly to her. Made their lives miserable.

And that's why in the end, Ryder decided he had to meet his father. Benjamin had controlled them for so long, his influence stretching long after his death. They were still hiding from his wrath. They were still denying themselves to live by his wishes. No more. And when Ryder told her that, Caroline softened.

Since then, Ryder and Charles made it a point to talk every week. That day was the first they met in person.

"What's he like?"

"You know what he's like," Ryder replied. "You hop in on our calls every chance you get."

I laughed. "I can't help it. I want to know how much of your personality is inherited. I'm preparing myself for the future mini-Ryders."

"Cute," he said. "Why were you late? What took you so long?"

"I thought I did a great job explaining the rules, but the pledges had a million questions for me."

"Yeah, must be tough," Ezra said. "Wouldn't blame you if you passed the job on to Blair, quit the sorority, and spent the rest of your time riding me. I can do just as good a job making you late."

I gave him a knowing look. "I don't doubt it." Jaxson, Ezra, and Ryder had been subtly and non-subtly suggesting I drop the Zetas and the program since one of their recruits almost stuck a pair of scissors through my brain and threw me out a window. Honestly, I could see why they weren't fans.

Although I knew how they felt, we talked about it and they understood how I felt too. This was my year of normal, fun, memories, and making a difference. Things I'd been denied since my freshman year of high school, and I was taking them back.

I wasn't worried about the program. Kessler initiated mandated therapy sessions. Aiden graduated and a new president took over Alpha Nu. My "don't give up the secret" challenge put an impressed glint in his eye. He was happy to go for it, but he was upping the stakes. Reveal the secret and receive a full-body shave from head to toe. The brothers hooted and hollered, yukking it up and proving I would never fully understand men.

"Everything is how I want it to be." I relaxed against Maverick, smiling at his arms securing me from behind. "I couldn't imagine it being any better than this."

"Everyone, can I have your attention, please?" Hudson led a confused Sofia to the middle of the room. "Thank you for being here to witness me make an arse of myself. Hopefully, she says yes anyway."

"Says yes? To what? What's going on?"

Hudson dropped to one knee. Sofia gasped, clapping a hand over her mouth.

"Sofia—"

"Yes!"

He blinked. "But I have a whole—"

"Yes."

"You haven't seen the ring—"

"Yes, yes, yes!" She tackled Hudson, kissing the crap out of him.

We clapped, laughed, cried (me), and cheered the happy couple as Hudson finally pulled out the ring.

"Okay," I said, smiling at my guys. "It can get more perfect. And I know that every single day I spend with you, it will."

Ten Years Later

"WE HAVE TOO MANY OF these."

Ryder marched into my studio carrying a twin under each arm. They were giggling their heads off at the fun trip. Ryder was missing a tie, piece of his shirt, and apparently a comb for those flyaways.

I stopped bouncing baby Jessie and shut off the music. "You're doing very well, Esme. You can take a break."

"Okay."

Esme stopped dancing and skipped to the table carrying her water bottle. Her next stop was to retrieve her baby sister. She took her out to get a snack.

Esme refused to be more than ten feet from the little girl. She cooed over the baby every chance she got, and it melted my heart seeing them together. Esme had her father's hair and Jaxson passed on his gold locks to his daughter, but the two of them looked so much like me, they could've been twins born years apart.

I flashed Ryder an amused smile. "What do we have too much of?"

"These." He brandished the twins. "Kids. Maybe we can return some of them."

They escaped his hold and ran shrieking from the dance studio—no doubt in search of the next mischief that'll drive their dads crazy.

"I'm afraid we've had them for too long," I said, opening my arms to him. "We got attached."

"Shit. You're right."

"What happened?"

"They ambushed me coming out the room. They have a game to see who can climb Mount Dad faster. How do they come up with this stuff?"

I was trying hard to contain my laughter, and it wasn't working. "I've got an idea of who passed on their mischievousness."

"Hey," he whispered, nipping my bottom lip. "Watch it, Moon."

Heat sizzled under my skin, following the path of his hands moving up my thighs to squeeze my ass. Ryder gifted me a mind-scrambling kiss—teasing my tongue to play with his. I broke away panting. Fifteen years we've been together, and Ryder still got my heart racing like it was hooked up to a car battery. *Vroom, vroom.*

"What are you thinking?"

I rested my hand on his heart. "I—"

"Mom. Dad," Esme called. "Lunch is ready."

We walked hand in hand out to the terrace. Me, Esme, and Ryder holding Jessie. Halfway there, Jessie decided to grab her dad's head and put it in her mouth. The deadpan look he gave me set me off again.

"What's the plan for this summer?" I asked. "The kids are out tomorrow. Should we take a trip up to visit your dad?"

"They're heading out to the lake for a week in July and invited us to join. We could do that and take another trip to Costa Rica."

I bit my lip thinking of our previous trips to Costa Rica. "Would that be with or without the kids?"

Jessie screeched—gnawing and pounding his face with her chubby little fists.

"And miss all this? Definitely with."

I swatted his backside, sending him out ahead of us.

The family—my family—was all gathered. Adam and Caroline talking at the head of the table. I still couldn't believe my little baby was seventeen years old and a blink from graduating. Esme was about to turn ten and was already a better dancer than me. Maverick and my twins, Gadget and Pixel as we called them, were five years old, double our trouble, and so much like their dad, I couldn't look at them and not see Maverick.

Maverick. I reached for his hand under the table.

Ten years since he joined the program, and in those years he's made incredible technological strides for Maverick Technologies and the partners he's cultivated over the years. All that and he still managed to be home to play with the kids and tuck them in after dinner.

"Sure you don't want us to transfer you to another school?" Jaxson asked Adam. "Just say the word."

"Thanks, Dad, but I can't. All my friends are at Breakbattle. Melody is there. I'd rather put up with the battle system than be the new kid my senior year."

"Yeah, I get it. Just make sure you let your mom know if it gets too much."

"I will."

Smiling, my foot caressed Jaxson's leg under the table. "What do you think about taking a trip to Costa Rica?"

My Jaxson could use a vacation. Interstellar Records was killing it. In the last decade, they've opened five studios around the country, and were signing more bands than ever. Their top artists were dominating the charts worldwide.

"Baby, wherever you're lying around in a bikini is where I'm going to be."

"Ugh, Dad," Adam complained. "Come on."

"All right." Ezra came out carrying a pizza pan. "Everyone should remember this. We ate it the last time we visited my dad. No one is allowed to say it's not as good as Grandpa's."

We appropriately oohed and aahed as he revealed the manakeesh—dough topped with ground beef, olive oil, and spices.

"It looks delicious, Daddy," Esme said.

"That's my girl. Pony for you."

"Yay!"

"Ezra," I said. "Don't joke about ponies."

"Who's joking?" He winked at Esme.

I shook my head. Ryder thought I implied the kids got their mischievousness from him, but it was a fifty-fifty split between him and Ezra. Even so, Ezra was amazing with the kids and just as amazing with me as he always was. Every week, he took me out for date night. A fancy dinner, sweet dessert, and talking about everything and anything. Most nights, we ended up booking in for a hotel where he gave breaking a hip a try. Thankfully we weren't old enough for that yet.

And Ryder.

Jessie had given up trying to eat him and nuzzled under his chin, drifting to sleep.

Ryder was my soul mate long before either of us knew it. He was the father he wished he had growing up. The boss who turned the company in the right direction. The son who brightened his mother's day. And the lover who made me feel wanted and beautiful every minute of every day.

Fifteen years, five kids, and six pets had passed by in a whirlwind of fighting, making up, laughter, tears, and special moments that defined our family. We had come so far, but I knew this was just our beginning.

"Ryder." I laid my chin on his shoulder and stroked Jessie's soft cheek. "Still think we have too many?"

"Nah. You were right. They've grown on me." He kissed her soft curls. "I wouldn't change a thing about our family."

"Well... I think we should change one thing."

He scrunched his brow. "What?"

"The number."

"The..."

Smiling, I rubbed my stomach. "I was thinking in a few months we should go from eleven to twelve."

"But how?"

"Baby Shea doesn't give a crap about birth control."

"Baby Shea?" A wide, beatific grin stretched across his face. "Are you sure?"

"I'm sure."

Ryder kissed the mess out of me, earning more groans from the kids, and laughs from us.

"I love you, Valentina. I never deserved you, but damn I won't give you up."

"Don't, baby." I held his hand to my stomach. "We're still a thousand years short of forever."

Adam Moon returns in Breakbattle Academy along with the strong and talented Zela Manning. Click here to start the series.[1]

---

1. http://mybook.to/Orientation

Keep In Touch

I hope you enjoyed reading the final book of Valentina's story.
If you want to chat with fellow Evergreen and Somerset lovers, join us
in my reader group, Ruby's Knights and Diamonds[1].
You can also join my mailing list for news, teasers, giveaways, and
more. Link up on Ruby's Mailing List[2].

---

1. https://bit.ly/3bNuCOq

2. https://www.subscribepage.com/rubyvincentpage

ABOUT THE AUTHOR

Ruby Vincent is a fan of all things enemies to lovers. Throw in twists, turns, and suspense, and she's hooked. She loves saucy heroines, bold alpha males, and weaving a tale where both get their happy ever after.